COOKIE CUTTER DADDY

JOE SATORIA

COOKIE CUTTER DADDY
JOE SATORIA

ISBN: 9798364670151

Satoria Publishing © 2022

www.JoeSatoria.com

Content: Daddy/little, low angst, holiday, dual POV.

Contents

ONE   1

TWO   10

THREE   20

FOUR   29

FIVE   42

SIX   53

SEVEN   63

EIGHT   73

NINE   83

TEN   92

ELEVEN   101

TWELVE   110

THIRTEEN   120

FOURTEEN   130

EPILOGUE   138

AUTHOR'S NOTE   143

About the Author   144

ONE

LELAND

This Christmas, I wished for one thing. An endless supply of gingerbread. I would take a bath in those tasty, sweet spices if I didn't think it would hurt.

There was another wish. I wanted a man. Specifically, someone who would role play with me. I knew who I wanted, but I didn't know if he wanted me back.

Standing in the cold, pulling my scarf snug around my neck, I stared through the misted glass window of *Marcus's Bakery* on Main Street. The window fogged with my breath. I was waiting for people to leave, but importantly, I was trying to spy on the owner. A gorgeous man with tattooed arms, and a smile that had me walking with a limp.

I'd been obsessing over him for years. And with good reason too. We'd kissed, several times, they were all drunk kisses at New Year's Eve parties.

Marcus Collins was an all-time love of mine. I always imagined him in a position of power over me. In my dreams, I gave him full control of my body. It made sense, especially when I was in my little space. He was only a couple years older than me. We went to the same high school. He was a senior when I was a freshman. I'd obsessed over him back then as well.

He didn't kiss me back in high school, obviously. But those drunk kisses, high on the holiday spirit were enough to fill me with hope. But I was never around after the holidays to see if he even remembered. This year was going to be different. I'd just moved back.

I couldn't spot him in the bakery, but it was busy.

A tap came at my shoulder. "Are you going to clean those windows?"

"Huh?" I spun on a foot, trying to hold my balance as I smacked a hand against the window, streaking it with gloved fingers. "I—"

"Leland," Marcus said, rolling his sleeves to show off his decorated tattooed arms. He wore a shirt and an apron. But he didn't look cold. "I was wondering when you'd show up. You missed the first snow last week."

"I—I—"

"Are you helping at the shelter again this year?" he asked.

"Your mom was in here the other day, and when I asked when you'd be back, she told me you were already back. Something about moving into an apartment here."

Busted. I told her not to tell anyone. Although I didn't specify who, so she'd probably been blabbing around all over town. I didn't blame her, I was *home* again, and she was proud of me.

Marcus invited me into the bakery at the side entrance from the alley. It led into the heart of the bakery; the boiling kitchen area.

"I was going to come in the other day, but—" my throat drying quickly. It felt like I was breathing heartbeats. "You know, I've been busy moving."

"No sweat," he chuckled. "I'm glad I caught you. I always—I—I always think about you during the holidays for some reason."

My throat felt like a desert. I need to be evacuated from this situation. "Fun."

"You should probably take you coat off; you look hot."

"Hot?"

"Yeah." He tugged at my sleeve. "These ovens blast out some high temperatures."

If it wasn't for the heat getting to me, it might've been the smells. It was a peppermint chocolate vanilla swirl heaven. "Sure." I removed my scarf first. "Christmas is usually when we see each other." Removing my coat to reveal the thick Christmas sweater beneath. I caught him smile. "Every time I—"

"So—oh," he started, interrupting me. "What were you going to say?"

Blushing, or still hot from my clothes, I pressed the back of my gloved hand against my cheeks to cool off. "I—I was gonna ask what you were doing. We should hang out some time, maybe. I don't know, you're probably busy. Don't mind me. I should focus on my new job."

Marcus shook his head, smiling. "One of the reasons I was asking about you, is because we have fun together."

He was right, but this time, I wasn't going to be leaving town. I'd be sticking around, so any fun we had would be clouded by a sea of confusion. "Yeah, sure, sure. I'm still unpacking, but I've got a couple of games consoles."

"I'm down for that," he said.

"Ok, well I'll—" I turned in the direction to exit.

He grabbed my arm. "Aren't you waiting until I close?" he asked. "For the leftovers to take to the shelter."

Right. The entire reason I was here.

I was out of place in the kitchen, watching as he cleaned down surfaces and shut down machines. He could have anyone he chose, man or woman. He owned a business, he smelled like heaven, and he was the perfect mix of sweet and spicy, just like gingerbread. Watching him take control of the bakery and the girl working on the cash register, he had Daddy vibes all over him.

Sitting on a stool in the clean kitchen, my coat on a

hanger, I waited for Marcus to finish up.

Flashes of memories from New Year's Eve last year bloomed behind my eyes. He made the move. His hand behind my head. The clock struck midnight, and our lips locked, our tongues touched. And that's where it ended, each year, like some weird Cinderella story, but there were no missing shoes, only kisses.

"Bethany just left," he said, walking back into the kitchen. He whipped a hand towel over his shoulder. "It's just the two of us." He chewed into a smile. "I see your grandma is still making sweaters?"

"She insisted," I told him. "So, I should probably get the food."

"I'm sure you can spare a couple minutes," he said. "I have some frosting leftover and it would be a shame for it to go to waste. Do you want to practice icing cookies?"

Oh, fudge. I really did want to be in this romantic moment with him. To him, it was two friends hanging out. To me, this was as intimate as handholding.

In previous year when I came by, it was just after closing, we shared a couple words, I grabbed the donations and left.

Marcus stood behind me, watching as I piped frosting on the Christmas tree cookie. His cool peppermint breath on my neck had my toes curled with pleasure. "You have a precise hand."

"It's my first time," I whispered, turning to him.

"You handle the bag like a pro."

A giggle escaped me. He didn't know just how well I could use my hands. "It's all about applying the right amount of pressure, right?"

He squeezed my shoulder. "And if I apply the right amount of pressure to you, what will happen?"

Gulping on the throbbing heartbeat in my throat, I quietly begged him to squeeze harder. "It might get— *sticky.*"

"Oh, really?"

As he applied pressure, I spun around. My hand growing tighter around the bag of frosting, popping the nozzle and shooting a thick line of icing between us. It landed on my face.

"Oopsie."

"You were right," he said, closing the space between our face. "That does look sticky." Extending his tongue and breathing his minty breath in my face, he licked at the frosting. "Damn, that's good. Whoever made it should get a raise."

Talking of things being raised, I backed up against the counter and shoved my erection into the waistband of my briefs. "Yeah, I—"

"Have a taste." He took a finger, scooping frosting from my cheek, he pressed it inside my mouth. His finger going further than it should, inserted almost to the knuckle. I'd sucked on plenty of candy canes to know I had no gag reflex. He was right though; the frosting was good. "I don't remember your tongue like that," he chuckled, removing his finger. "I mean—"

Fussing with my hands, I wiped the frosting from my face. I was trying to avoid the topic; I didn't know what he was talking about. Unless, and of course, he was talking about our kisses. "I should probably be at the shelter soon."

"Let me get the rest of your face." He applied a cold wet cloth to my skin, cleaning it off. "I guess now we know for next time about pressure control. And if you squeeze too hard, it might just explode in your face." His words were soft, like ASMR, it tingled the back of my neck and forced me to gulp hard, tasting the pure sugar he'd got me to suck from his finger.

Out of words, I wanted to invite him over now, the sparks between us were weird. Sober sparks. I thought it had been the New Year's Eve champagne that got us.

Marcus had prepared a large basket of baked goods that hadn't sold. "Will I see you tomorrow?"

"Tomorrow," I mumbled, grabbing my winter coat. "Probably."

"You have my number, right?"

"I have a new phone, actually, so no."

He smiled, grabbing a Sharpie from a pen pot on the metal counter. "In case you need any help unpacking, or just want to hang." He took the back of my hand and wrote his number. "I don't have many plans for the holidays. So hit me up."

"I will," I said, unsure if I would. "I'm sure you'll be swamped with family."

"My folks are in Florida, and my sister moved to the West Coast, so I'm—I'm not swamped, actually."

Something in me, it took total control. "If that's the case, why don't you come to the shelter with me, and then we could—we—we—"

"We could go back to yours and play games?" he asked.

It was a friend date, although I was the one who'd suggested video games. I could manage a friend date. I was in no place for an actual date, and my apartment was mostly in boxes still. "Sure!"

"I'll get out of this, and lock up then," he said, pulling at his apron.

I convinced myself we were just friends and nothing more. Because that's just what this was. Two friends who kissed a couple times, and one of them was gay, and the other one was heteroflexible—clearly. I'd only known him to have girlfriends, and I knew better than to chase after straight men.

Out in the snow and cold, we walked together down to the local shelter. The crunch of snow underfoot and the silence in the air was nice. Cars drove slowly and everyone seemed to wave at Marcus. Everyone knew him, they loved him.

"Are you glad to be back?" he asked, striking up conversation.

"I am. I always think it's going to be different coming home, and then it's just the same," I said.

He scoffed. "Hey, things change around here," he said. "They put a new bell in the clock tower. It was a whole event; they wrote about it in the local paper." His voice petered off into laughter. "I made these cookies for the event, and before I decorated them, they looked like—well, dicks, basically. I never realized how much it looked like a dick before."

I giggled. "I was in New York. We don't get the Hinton newspaper. I don't think we get any New Hampshire papers."

"People change too," he said, quietly.

"People do change. I changed," I said. "I changed from loving New York, to never wanting to go back. I'm glad my dad could give me a job here. And I'm glad they pushed me into becoming an accountant. Although sometimes I hated looking at numbers. But then I reminded myself that it's better than being stressed in the city. Plus, everything is way cheaper here."

Marcus took hold of my arm. "I meant me," he said. "I've changed. I'm surprised you never noticed it. I came out as bisexual at the start of the year."

Pausing in shock, I was pulling everything into question.

So, was this a video game friend date? Or more?

TWO

MARCUS

It started three years ago. The first time I saw Leland since high school. I didn't really see him in high school. He was a nerdy freshman, and I was on my way to college. But it turns out that college wasn't for me. I went to culinary school and opened a bakery.

Leland came into the bakery that Christmas, asking for donations to the shelter. His family were big in community. I'd been donating to the shelter for a while. It was the first time I saw him when I wondered about myself. His odd nervous shuffling and the way his fingers intertwined. I started baking more just so I had more to give him when he came to collect.

It all culminated in a kiss at midnight in the town square. We never talked about it. I didn't have any opportunity to talk. He always left town the very next day.

We did it the year after, and again last year. I'd planned on telling him I liked him. But it would never work. He lived in a different state. I was still living in our hometown. I was trying to figure out my feelings then, but I knew them now. It only took me until I turned twenty-nine to actually search the internet for answers to my feelings. I discovered more than I bargained for.

He didn't say anything but smile and nod when I came out to him. I probably shouldn't have blurted it at him like that. I could've waited until we were at his apartment.

Leland was living above his father's accountancy office. It was a fully functioning apartment with a kitchen, bathroom, and a large bedroom-living area. It was nicer than my place above the bakery. But I suppose that's what I got when I was desperate to buy a building without doing much research.

"You need a hand unpacking?" I asked as I stood in the middle of the space, seeing the box towers. I pulled off my winter coat.

"I invited you over to play video games," he said, his cheeks bright red. He took my coat. "I'll order pizza."

"I can make pizza," he said.

"No, that's fine."

"Seriously." I placed a hand on his shoulder. "I can make

a good pizza." From my touch over the sweater, I gave him a squeeze. It came out of nowhere, like my brain took over and I was thinking of gently kneading dough.

Leland cleared his throat. "Confession, I haven't bought groceries yet, so I—I've mostly been going to my parents' place for meals. And takeout, obviously." He seemed to lean into my touch. "What type of pizza do you like?"

"Pepperoni," I said. "Or something spicy."

His eyes widened. "I—I don't eat pork." He placed a hand at his stomach. "But I'll phone and see if they can do a half-and-half."

"Great, and I'll look through your games."

"The TV is behind those boxes; you might have to push them aside."

There were boxes everywhere, navigating them like I was in some distribution center. I pushed a stack of boxes aside to reveal the widescreen TV on the stand with the consoles laid out next to each other. I was in awe of the collection, and not only that, but the stack of games on the rack beside the TV.

Pushing the boxes to have full view of the screen. The top box toppled, spilling out on the floor. "Crap," I grumbled, staring at what I'd done. I looked to see Leland on the phone with his back to me. "Just clothes," I noted in a whisper. But it wasn't just clothes. They were adult onesies, with patterns and themes on them. I dipped to my knees and pushed them back into the fallen box. There were at least ten onesies, some of them with little teddies attached to the zippers.

Turning, Leland stood behind me. "I—uh—so—"

"You don't have to explain," I said. "Everyone should feel comfy in their home."

"Yeah, but, they—" He was searching for something to say. His shoulders sinking and his brows dipping in the middle of his forehead. "I'm donating them."

"Oh ok." I nodded. "I think they're cute. I personally can't sleep in any clothes. Naked, all the way." I paused, reflecting in realization about how freely I'd volunteered that information. I suppose it was one way I could get him to picture me naked. "So, these are the games.

"There's a lot."

"Um—do you want a beer?"

"Sure."

Leland went into overdrive going through the games with me, mostly picking out and putting aside his favorite multiplayer games. It took us until the pizza arrived before we even decided on a game.

He'd pulled out two giant beanbags for us to sit on. We used the top of a box as a makeshift table for the pizza and beer.

"Racing games are my favorite," Leland said.

"Racing games are my favorite," I said, toying with him.

Feigning a gasp, Leland playfully whacked my hand. "Copycat," he said. "I hope you like losing, because I always come first."

"Ok, let's make it interesting then, since you're talking a big game." I didn't know what I was doing. I was making it up as I went along. This was the first time I'd ever flirted with a guy, and for all I knew, he didn't even see this as flirting. "Loser does a forfeit." Ok, that was one way to get the ball rolling and see where this could go.

"Forfeit," he said, snapping his fingers in the air with sass. "I was gonna suggest that, but I thought you'd chicken out."

"Chicken," I scoffed, grabbing a slice of pizza. "Get ready to eat your words. Who are you gonna play as?"

Leland already had his character selected, one of the princess characters. I chose the big aggressive looking dude with horns. If he looked that menacing, then he was bound to do some damage.

The race was about to start. I held the controller in my hand, toying with the idea of failing on purpose. I wondered what my forfeit would be.

I was cocky and confident to think I would win. I didn't play games much, but it was in my nature to want to impress and be cocky. I couldn't help it. I was in overdrive to show him I was cool.

His eyes were intense, staring at the screen, powering his thumb and fingers down on all the buttons. I didn't have to fail on purpose, he was way ahead of me.

"You've got to get the power ups," he said.

"I'm trying. I think you gave me a faulty car. I don't think this one passed all its tests."

Leland let out another little giggle. "It's ok to lose," he said. "But don't blame your decision."

It didn't take long before the race ended, and his side of the screen flashed with the first-place badge and mine was somewhere near the end.

"I'm just a little rusty," I told him, grabbing a slice of pepperoni pizza. "My hand needs warming up to really press those buttons like you did."

His smile was big. I could see him wanting to run around screaming about winning, but he didn't. He stared into my eyes before giving one heavy-handed clap. "Obviously," he began. "This means you have to do a forfeit."

Chewing on the pizza, I nodded. I wanted him to test me. I wanted to feel like there was something between us still. All those kisses, and I still wanted more. Maybe not with a mouthful of pizza, but eventually, I did. "So," I said, after swallowing. "Give it your best shot, what do you want me to do?"

He tapped fingers on his chin theatrically. "Maybe we could turn it into truth or dare."

"I'm down for that," I said, jumping at the chance. "Dare."

"Um. I—I dare you to shove the rest of the pizza slice in your mouth. All at once."

The pizza slice had a single bite taken out of it. It wasn't impossible. "Easy," I told him.

"Then do it," he teased.

I folded the slice up and shoved it in my mouth, chewing as it went inside. I watched as his eyes opened wider, staring at the act. I made sure not to leave a single drop of sauce on my hands or around my lips, licking it away. I finally swallowed. "Next time, I'll choose truth."

He snickered. "So, you expect to lose again?"

That wasn't what I'd meant to say, but having seen the way he played, it was probably what was realistically going to happen. We played another game, and it came in as another loss. Leland looked smugger now, taking a sip of his beer and smacking his lips.

"Ok, truth," I said.

"Truth, truth, truth," he said as he tapped his fingers along the neck of the beer bottle. "Why did you stay in Hinton?"

That was an easy one. "I like it here. I know people here."

"But have you never wanted to leave?"

"I think the rules of truth or dare say it's only one question," I said, my smile aching, but I couldn't help smiling around him. "To answer you, no. I've never wanted to leave. I'd love to travel more, but I love to bake, and I get to do that every single day."

He nodded. "I love that."

"What about you?" I asked. "Why did you come back?"

The cogs were turning. He grabbed a slice of pizza, stopping himself from speaking. There had to have been a story behind it, somewhere. I just knew there was something to it. I was pleased he was back.

"You don't have to answer," I told him. "But I accept coming back to eat from my bakery as an answer."

He blushed, nodding. "Fine," he said through the muffle of food. "I came back because of those gingerbread cookies."

"You should've said. I would've brought some." Perhaps an apartment warming gift, something to scent the air with other than pizza and beer. "I'm glad you're back."

"Oh, yeah, and why's that?" he asked.

"I like you," I blurted. I couldn't take it back. "I mean— like, you know, I think we get along really well."

Leland's face turned beet red. "As a friend then," he said. "Great."

"Sure." I didn't want to dig any deeper, but what my brain wanted, and what my mouth wanted were very different things. "Or as more than friends."

"I—I—I don't think we've known each other long enough to be *best friends*," he chuckled.

I knew he knew what I meant, and now I was coming off on him way too strong. "Sorry."

There was a moment of quiet when we both sipped beer and avoided eye contact.

"Usually, I'm the one putting my foot in my mouth," he

said, barely audible over the sound from the game. "I obviously like you."

"Ok, so if I beat you on this next race, then maybe we can hang out some more," I said.

Butting his teeth over his lips to force back his smile, his eyes lingered, squinting at me. "Are you saying that, so you'll make me lose the race?"

"What? No!" I slapped a hand on my knee. That was exactly what I was hoping would happen. "But would it work?"

"Maybe. There's just one issue really."

"What's that?" I asked, my mouth dry with nerves.

"I can't lose on purpose," he whispered. "If someone wants something, they have to take it."

A shiver ran up my spine. "What you're saying is, you want to be dominated?"

"I'm not *not* saying that," he snickered, placing a hand over his mouth. "Do you think you can?"

Puffing out my chest with a deep breath, I gave it a pound with a fist. Amping myself up. "I can, and I will take that first place from you."

I watched as he twitched and grinned, the same spark of a shiver that had gone through me was now in him. "Good," he said. "Because I'm probably gonna be super busy, so if you wanna hang out some more, you're gonna have to win."

Somehow, I knew that was a lie, not the wanting to hang out part, but him being super busy. Either way, I was ready to play, and I was playing to win.

THREE

LELAND

I let him win. Eventually.

It took several races, but I let him win.

The pizza was eaten. The beers were emptied. Our eyes strained and ached.

He left once it got late, telling me he had to be awake early for the bakery tomorrow.

We almost kissed when he was leaving. It was strange. There were parts of the evening when I thought he might've just taken me and thrown me onto my bed, and then other parts of the evening when I thought he was going to ask my father if he could start dating me.

I climbed into bed with Marcus's face playing on a loop

through my mind. I was in my all-white onesie with light blue snowflakes printed on it. And I cuddled close to my stuffie. A washed-out pink pig named Oinky. It was why I didn't eat pork, so no bacon or sausages, and definitely no pepperoni. I'd had Oinky since I was nine, and he slept in bed with me every single night.

A wave of cold air woke me. I barely even realized I'd been to sleep until snapping my eyelids open. My eyes were dry and aching. The air conditioning was on automatically. It was the middle of winter, and I couldn't figure out how to program it.

Laid still in bed, I stared at the ceiling and yawned. I still had a few weeks before I was set to work at the firm downstairs. It cut my commute time way down, but I'd still have to wake up earlier than I'd like. My first thought after that was Marcus, wondering if he was awake, and imagining how he smelled. It wasn't much of a leap for my brain, since I could almost smell him from being here last night.

It was Wednesday, and there was just over a week until Christmas.

Showering and dressing in another winter sweater, I was pulled into my little space. The want to sit in front of colorful cartoons and scribble mercilessly on pages with a new set of crayons was strong. That wasn't always my little space, sometimes it was drinking from my piggy shaped sippy cup and eating with my plastic plate and cutlery, all pink with piggies on them.

Christmas was the one time of year when everything triggered the little space in me. It was a comfort blanket from adult responsibilities. I dashed through memories of the holidays. Every holiday was covered in blinking colorful lights and tall fir trees, decorated with tinsel, and even though the tinsel was scratchy, I almost always tried to wear it as a boa around my shoulders.

I arrived at the family home just in time for brunch. I was given the option of moving back home, but that seemed like a step away from having my space. I parked in the drive and took in the scenery of the house. Wondering if there was anything spare for me to take back to my apartment.

The family home had inflatables out front and a sleigh on the roof. None of them were turned on just yet, but in the evening when it got dark, they lit up the house with sound, movement, and light.

"Is that my baby?" Grandma screamed from the front door. She was wrapped tight in a knitted shawl and threatening to come outside barefoot in the snow.

"Grandma." I hugged her. She kept hold of me, sniffing.

"You need to come visit me at my home," she said. "It's difficult for a woman of my age to get around town. You know I've got a bad hip."

With an arm around her, I walked with her into the living room. "Mom," I called out. "Grandma almost got out of the house. She's not wearing any shoes."

Grandma clicked her tongue and smacked her lips.

"Who needs shoes?" she scoffed. "I've been standing at that door for five minutes waiting for you."

"Grandma, I only saw you the other day."

We walked to the sofa where her knitting needles and basket of yarn were waiting midway through a project.

"Sometimes it feels like forever," she said, taking her seat. And as I took my coat off, she cooed at me. "Is that one of mine?"

"Yeah, you made it for me."

"I know," she chuckled. "I'm old, not senile. I just—I just need my glasses on, that's all." She patted the seat. "I've no idea where I put them."

"Mom," my mom said, walking in from the dining room. "Your glasses are on your head." She approached me, taking my coat. "How are you, hon?"

"I can hang my coat," I said.

"If people did everything for themselves, what would I do?" She shook her head in feigned shock. "Look, Mom, Leland is wearing the sweater you knitted him."

I missed my family when I lived away. I only saw them during the holidays, and if they came to visit. It was nice when they came, because I got to take them to see shows on Broadway. I suppose a bit of why I moved back was to be closer to family. Another reason was a less stressful job. It would still be in accounting, but everything was cheaper, and my dad owned the apartment I was living in now, so rent was almost a nonissue.

Dad was in his home office upstairs. Mom was making brunch and grandma was knitting as *Judge Judy* played on the TV.

"Hey son," Dad said as I knocked on his office door. "How's the apartment?"

I envied his office. It looked like a small library. It's where he spent a lot of time during my childhood, and to spend time with him, I would sit on the chair in the corner of his room facing his desk and I'd read while he worked. Or at least looked like he was working.

I sat in the same spot I did as a child. "The apartment is fine, still figuring everything out."

"It's been a while since anyone lived up there," he said, looking at me from above his computer screen. "You have everything on, right?" His brows pinched with concern. "I don't want you freezing to death in that apartment."

"Everything is fine. Well, there is the aircon that comes on in the morning, but I'll figure it out," I told him. The smell of pancakes and coffee traveled through the air, reminding me why I came upstairs. "Mom said she's got pancakes on the griddle if you want any. She said you only had a coffee for breakfast."

Dad chuckled, patting a hand on his stomach. "You know, they're doing the production in the town square for the Christmas fair. Jenny asked me to play Santa," he said.

"And you turned it down?"

"What do you think?" he said, continuing to laugh. "I'm

not that old, and I'm only a little gray. Your mother found it hilarious. I think she asked Jenny to offer me it. Plus, your brother's being roped in to play an elf with his girlfriend."

The Christmas fair was the weekend before Christmas. They had stalls set up in the square, horse and carriage rides, people caroling, and the all-important Santa's grotto. "I'm looking forward to it," I said. "Who did they get to play Santa then?"

"I think they got the football coach from your brother's high school," he said.

"Oh, where is Harry?"

He gave me a shrug. My younger brother, Harry, was a senior in high school. We were opposites of each other. I loved being at home, reading, playing games and spending time gossiping. I think it might've been my love of sitting by my grandma with a juice box while she gossiped about her friends that ultimately outed me as being gay.

I didn't spend too much time at the house with my folks. I had a lot of unpacking left to do, and I'd been procrastinating over it with video games. And before I left, my mom gave me the order to visit the bakery again, almost like she was trying to set me and Marcus up. She only ever had kind things to say about him, everyone in town did.

Once home, I realized I'd lied to myself. I fell for the oldest trick in the book with the idea that once I got a little dopamine in my body, I'd be productive. It turns out, I just wanted to keep on that dopamine track of playing games until I saw the evening darkness creep in behind the television screen. This time, I'd been building a farm where I could live with all my animals. But I only had pigs.

My stomach rumbled. The only thing I'd eaten today were those pancakes my mom made, shaped like a bear with three circles. She always did it, telling me that's how I liked them when I was a boy. I still did like them that way.

Looking at my wristwatch as I raced around the apartment to find my other shoe in the sea of chaos, I realized I was going to be late picking the leftovers up from the bakery.

The bakery was still open by the time I'd weighed myself down with my winter coat and boots.

Marcus stood behind the counter, wiping the surface. He spotted me staring in and a large smile appeared on his face before he gestured for me to go around the back.

"I was supposed to stop by earlier," I said, immediately as the door opened.

"It's no problem," he said, tugging my coat for me to enter. "I was—I was actually waiting for you."

"You were?" I asked. Somewhat ashamed and partly embarrassed he'd been waiting. "I'm sorry."

"You owe me, since I won the game last night," he said.

"Huh?"

He held up a plastic shopping bag. "Are we still on for tonight?" He handed me the bag.

Looking inside, it didn't look like the leftover pastries.

"I—um—"

"It's for pizza," he said. "I told you I could make pizza, so I bought ingredients. Oh, and I have gingerbread, 'cause you said you like that."

The sudden heat hit my cheeks. This sounded more like a date *date* than a friend date, and like usual, I was oblivious. I tried butting my teeth over my lips to keep myself from giggling. "You're serious?" I asked. "You can make pizza?"

"I can do one better," he said. "I can make the best pizza you'll have ever tasted." He held his hand up, extending his little finger out to me. "Pinky promise."

"I—um—I have to get to the shelter first, and my mom enlisted me to serve her beef stew," I told him. "But—but I'm down for pizza and gingerbread." My stomach grumbled louder, and the corners of my mouth were already salivating.

He took the bag from me with a beaming smile. "I'll bring this over later then," he said. "The pastries are in here." He tapped a hand on a box. "I might've been up earlier than usual baking up a storm. I—I couldn't sleep last night, after being beaten at that game."

A snort came out. "How about we play a different game tonight?"

Marcus held his hands up and wiggling his thumbs. "But I've been practicing with thumb exercises."

"We'll see later. Thank you. I appreciate it." I grabbed the box, needing to get out of the bakery and into the biting cold air outside, something to calm my blushing skin.

"How long until I should come over?" he called out to me as I left, following me to the door.

"An hour," I told him, escaping off down the street, the giggle stuck in my throat. Tonight, I was going to have pizza made by the man I'd been crushing on for years, and it was probably a date *date*.

FOUR

MARCUS

I got to his apartment early, forgetting I couldn't wait in a hallway. I stood in the cold, my beanie snug on my head and a scarf wrapped tight around my neck. Carrying the bag of ingredients, feeling proud and pleased. If there was one thing I loved doing, it was showing off, and cooking for the people I liked.

Leland was someone I liked. He was peculiar in the best way. I'd always wanted to go further with him to see where it would go and what would happen. And he gave me butterflies. Even now, as I spotted him stomping his feet through the snow on the sidewalk. His smile illuminated in the streetlight. He waved, noticing me, followed by tripping and stumbling to his knees in the snow.

"I'm ok," he called out, dusting himself off. He stood like a scarecrow.

"Come on," I said. "People are watching."

"Right," he shouted back. "So, I should be slow. I don't want to embarrass myself *again* in front of everyone."

The odd person peered out of their window and watched as we called out to each other. I didn't want to see him fall *again*, but I also wanted him to move faster. There was only so much cold my gloved hands could take.

He reached me, and with instinct, I hugged him. It was a long hug, almost like trying to cuddle for warmth. I wasn't against it, but I didn't want to get ahead of myself. We could cuddle for warmth some other time, when it came naturally.

"I'm starving," he said, digging around inside his coat for keys. "I had the tiniest bit of the stew my mom brought, but only because she forced me to. I told her about tonight. You, me, homemade pizza."

My teeth chattered. "Then I guess it was a good decision for me to make the dough and sauce at the bakery." I had time to kill, and I was just as hungry. All we needed to do was roll the dough, add the sauce, the toppings, and bake.

Reaching his apartment, it was only a touch warmer than it had been outside.

"Ugh," he sighed. "I was messing with the settings on the blasted thing earlier. It's from like ancient times, I swear." Leland stood in front of the thermostat on the wall, tapping it. "I don't know if I turned the heat off."

I chuckled, it was all I could do, seeing his cute face in all that confusion. "As someone who has to deal with a faulty heater at the bakery, I can take a look at it," I told him.

"You know, I told my dad I had everything figured out except for the air conditioning."

"Air conditioning," I blurted. "You do realize it's winter, what would you need cold air for?"

"Nooooo," he giggled. "That's the problem. It's on a timer or something, and I don't know how to shut it off. And—and I think when I was playing with the settings, I must've knocked something else off instead." His face and cheeks flushed hues of pink. At least one of us looked warm.

With the older buildings in the town, it was easy for things to get confusing. Although it seemed that his apartment had some nice upgrades to it. I hadn't realized yesterday since it had been nice and toasty, plus, I was distracted by being around him. Once I figured out he'd been using the wrong settings and instead of turning the air conditioner off, he turned the heating off and decided to pump in ice cold air. I didn't tell him what he'd done, I could see how stressed out he was.

"My hero. It's all fixed then?" he asked, removing his coat. "I wonder how long it'll take to warm up. I suppose you're not going anywhere so you can reverse it and put the air con on in summer, right?"

"I suppose," I chuckled. "I don't plan on leaving town. And once I've got the oven on, it should help warm the place up." At least, that's how it worked in the bakery, but there were several ovens there. I should've enjoyed the ice in the air since I was used to being blasted by heat.

Unpacking the bag of ingredients on the counter with Leland's warm presence behind me. "Why is it so big?" he asked.

"It's a grower," I said in a knee-jerk reaction.

He prodded the plastic wrap over the dough in the bowl. "It looks like a shower to me."

"That's the yeast," I explained. "It makes things expand and get bigger. Plus, I made enough for us to have many pizzas, if we choose. I don't know how hungry you are, but I've barely eaten. And I've been on my feet all day." There I went, divulging too much about my life.

A gargling grumble came from Leland's belly, muffled by layers of clothes. It was answered by a grumble from my stomach, almost like they were communicating.

He snickered. "So, what can I do to help?"

I opened the cupboards and drawers. "Rolling pin, or a tube of some kind, and—" Staring into the cupboard, I saw plastic cutlery, plates, and bowls. There had little pink pigs all over them. I bypassed it and found what I was looking for. The rolling pin. Surprised he had one.

"Ok, just an FYI on what I said yesterday," he said, letting out an audible gulp. "I don't eat pork. Not because of religion or anything, but—but you saw the teddy earlier on my bed, I know you did, and—the kid's plates. I love pigs. I just can't eat them."

A real moment of raw emotion, the heat radiated from him as he spoke.

"That's ok," I said. "I'll eat the pepperoni. You can have—"

"Just cheese is fine," he said. "That's what I usually get."

Leland continued to watch over my shoulder as I sprinkled a little flour on the counter and rolled a small ball of dough out into a circle. "Where did you learn to do that?"

"Something I picked up," I said. "I studied in Italy for a couple months. Amazing food." And it really was, thinking about the food I ate and enjoyed while now starving felt like I was going through torture.

"I've never been, but I'd love to," he said. "I went on a school trip to Paris and another to London in high school."

I gave Leland a little control as he rolled out dough into a unique circle. He looked pleased, before wiping a hand at his face, dotting his nose with flour. I wiped it away with my thumb, it was another instinct, and I was beginning to feel the flutters in my belly intensify.

"Sauce!" he said. "Is it in that jar?"

"Yes, yes. I said I made sauce. I had time to kill."

"Yesssss!" he grabbed the jar of tomato sauce. It was a mix of tomato, water, olive oil, and herbs. I could've gone store-bought, but I also wanted us to make it together. In a way, we did. "I think it's stuck," he said, pouting as he tried to open the jar.

I opened it in with a single twist.

"I guess all those years playing lacrosse helped," he said.

"Wait—wait, you remember me playing lacrosse?"

He looked away, blinking rapidly at what I was saying. "I—I remember seeing your team picture."

"I think you attended a couple of games," I teased.

"Can you blame me? Seeing guys tackling each other did something for me." He immediately cupped a hand over his mouth. "I mean—well, you know what I mean."

I wanted to kiss him right there and then, but I had some restraint, at least. "It was a lot of fun," I said. "Now, the trick with the sauce is not to put too much on the dough. If there's too much, it will become too wet. So, I'll add a couple blobs to yours, then you can spread it out."

He did just as I said, nodding his head with the instruction and then looking back at me for approval, in a way, it almost reminded me of training an apprentice. Except, I wasn't being as mean as I would to them, and I would've had him learn the hard way about food ratios.

We finished the pizzas with cheese, and I added slices of pepperoni. By that point, the apartment warmed up considerably and we were able to sit on the beanbags and relax without shivering.

"Marcus," he said, softly, tugging on my beanbag to pull me closer.

"Yeah?" I shuffled closer, knowing he couldn't move me without help.

I stared deep into his green eyes and watched him gently wet his lips with the tip of his tongue. His mouth opened to speak, and before he could get a word out, I had a hand on the back of his head and my face against his. We kissed, our tongues connecting in a way they hadn't since the New Year's Eve party.

Fireworks went off inside my mind. Leland sat on my lap, getting closer, his hands exploring my body, lifting my sweater, he placed them on my stomach. I copied his movements and hoped not to do anything wrong. I'd never been with a guy before, no matter how much I'd wanted Leland before.

A rumble tingled against my fingers as I felt Leland's belly.

"Oops," he giggled, pulling away.

"I—I think our pizza is ready." I said as the strong smell scented the air. It was nice, mixed with the heat both of our bodies had been generated.

Leland stood, immediately turning away from me.

I adjusted the erection to my waist band and stood, seeing him pull his hand from his trousers, seemingly doing the same thing.

The pizzas were done to perfection. We sat on the beanbags and placed the pizzas on plates, his on the adorable pink plastic one, and mine on ceramic. Leland grabbed beers and we clinked glasses, staring at each other. I wondered where today was going, and how far we might go. I had condoms, at least two in my wallet. Unless they expired, I hadn't had sex in many months.

"Before we go any further, I—"

"Want to say grace?" I asked.

"No, I—this is about me," he said, closing his eyes, he inhaled a deep breath. "But between us, before it goes any further, I should probably tell you that I'm a—"

"A little," I said.

Leland's eyes lit up. "How—"

"I put a couple things together. The onesies, the plastic plate, cutlery, and I think I saw a sippy cup, and of course, the teddy."

He let out the breath he'd propped himself up with and smiled, grabbing a slice of pizza. "Ok, and—and what do you think about that?"

I grabbed a slice of pizza and took the time while eating to think of an answer. "When I started exploring my sexuality, I came across a lot of things, like little play and I—"

"What did you think about it?"

"I never really did think about it," I admitted. "I'd always been attracted to the sort of innocent play, the big eyes and pouts, and the way you had child-like excitement. I remember New Year's Eve two years ago, watching the wonder on your face as fireworks went off above us."

Leland stared at me; his lips pinched together.

"I'd love to know more about it, and about you too."

He swallowed the pizza in his mouth. "I'd love to see where we were headed earlier with those kisses," he said. "And—maybe if you call me a good boy, I'll show you what I can do."

My hunger was outweighed by my horniness. I said those two magic words to him. "Good boy." And he pounced on top of me. The throb of my erection grew harder in my waistband, almost aching against the band. "What do you want to call me?"

"Daddy," he whispered in my ear.

Something feral took over as I wrapped my arms around Leland's back and picked him up. "Say it again."

"Daddy," he moaned.

On the bed, I laid him out and undressed him down to his underwear, which he quickly placed a hand to cover so I didn't see the bulge. I didn't care about seeing it, all I cared about was connecting our bodies. I undressed, pulling my clothes off as fast as I could, keeping my underwear on, a pair of tight black briefs with my cock stuffed to the right as if it was trying to direct traffic. Leland watched, biting his bottom lip.

Crawling on top of him, feeling the heat radiate on our skin as it touched was heaven. Both our chests rose and dipped with deep breaths. I hadn't thought much about what he looked like under those large Christmas sweaters.

All I cared about was being close.

We continued to kiss and roll around. Our hands were busy feeling every inch of skin and muscle. His chest was soft, shaved, and he smelled like sweet soap. His fingers traced the tattoos up my arms to discover the ones hidden on my chest.

"I want you inside me," he whispered after our cocks had been squeezed together inside underwear, the only part of each other we hadn't seen or explored yet. We rolled over. He was on top, going down my body.

"I want you," I said. "I have—condoms in my wallet."

Leland's fingers teased at my waistband. "Can I ask one question first?"

"Yeah, anything."

"Am I your first?"

My tongue squeezed between my teeth. It wasn't like I was a virgin, but he was my first guy. "Yeah."

He beamed, smiling back at me as he climbed off the bed. I wanted to know what he was thinking. Maybe he liked that he was my first. He grabbed my wallet and pulled out the two condoms. Examining them, he looked at the date. "I'm not pressuring you or anything, am I?"

I scoffed. "Are you kidding?" Propping myself up on my elbows, I shook my head. "I was trying not to pressure you."

Leland bounced on the bed, jumping until he sat just below my underwear. "Can I take it out?" he asked, prodding my erection.

"Please do." I laid back, watching Leland pull back my underwear to reveal my cock. It wasn't the biggest, but it was thick, and currently as hard as a jawbreaker. "You can taste it," I said, as he'd look at me, almost asking permission with his eyes.

His mouth was magic, he worked it with his tongue before taking it in his mouth. He moaned on it, the vibrations from the back of his throat against my tip had my toes curling.

"My turn," I said, knowing if he went on any longer, I would bust a nut. I'd watched plenty of porn exploring my sexuality, and I always imagined my first time with a guy. But it was different to how it was on video; my skin was electric, and there was no calming it.

His cock was a little bigger than mine, but skinnier. I took as much of it as I could into my mouth, but I discovered quickly a gag reflex. I went down to lick his balls and seek out his hole. Pulling his knees to his chest and his legs in the air, he presented it to me like a prize.

I ate his ass with the same hunger I went into attacking pizza.

Leland's hand on mine, as he ruffled his other through my hair. "Fuck me," he said, softly.

The fiery tingles up my body had me in a chokehold. I tore open a condom and slipped it over my cock. With the excess lube from the condom, I pressed it against his hole. His eyes opened wider, and his teeth sank deeper into his bottom lip. Exploring it with just the tip of my cock was difficult as his hole was tight.

"Use your finger first," he said.

A single finger with the lube went inside, I gently pushed in a second finger. Leland's head went back against the pillow as he moaned. I knew my cock was at least four fingers smushed together in girth. It excited me to see how he'd react. I'd opened him a little now, and the tip of my cock was easier to insert.

Leland's hand scrunched the bedsheets.

Slowly, I pushed on my hips and went deeper.

"Fuck me," he said through a gasp.

Pressing my hands against his inner thighs, pushing his knees on his chest, I fucked him, back and forth like I was following our collective connected heartbeats.

Switching positions, side by side, Leland's back against my chest and my cock deep in his ass. He took some control of the rhythm.

"You like that?" I asked, my lips at his ear as I played with his nipples.

He increased with the rhythm, moving back and forth on my cock. He didn't realize how close I was to cumming. I just wanted to stay inside him, holding the erection as we cuddled. I ran my hand down his body. He was ticklish, and moving faster, back and forth.

"Oh, baby," I whispered. "Oh—oh—I—"

"I'm gonna cum," he said, grabbing my hand and

wrapping it around his cock.

I jerked him as he continued to move faster.

He lasted seconds, his cock pulsing in my hand, cumming everywhere, and his hole clenched tight around my cock. I came, filling the condom up inside him.

We didn't move. My hold on him grew stronger. I didn't want to leave the moment, or the ecstasy running a dopamine high through me. I'd never been happier in my entire life.

FIVE

LELAND

I didn't want to leave his warm embrace. I didn't want to be the one to break the connection our bodies were sharing moments after we both came. That to me was a special moment, but I'd made a mess, and there was cum all over my belly.

Cleaning myself off in the bathroom, wondering if what I thought just happened really had. I still felt him inside me. It was like a dream, and I didn't want to wake from it. I wrapped my bottom half in the towel from the bathroom. Marcus was on the bed; he'd put his underwear back on.

"That was nice," he said, sat up against the headboard. I took in the tattoos on his arms and chest.

"I think I'm hungrier now than I was earlier," I said, nodding at the pizzas on the cardboard box.

He smacked a hand at his belly. "Same. And I kinda like cold pizza."

"Really? Me too! You know, I've had so much trauma from eating hot pizza. This one time, I didn't think my mouth would recover, and I've put some—" I paused, the excitement had taken over me. "Some questionable things in my mouth," I continued with an attempt at being calm.

Marcus smiled, he didn't make me feel weird or self-conscious, the total opposite in fact, it was warm, and now I knew what his full body embrace felt like, I wanted more of it.

We sat on the beanbags again, Marcus insisting I sit between his legs to share body heat. I jumped at the chance, cuddling my back against his chest.

"I wasn't lying earlier," he said.

With a mouthful of pizza, I hummed trying to get my words out. I was glad he didn't have a direct view of my face and the way my cheeks were puffed with food, like a hamster storing seeds and nuts.

He chuckled. "Were you asking me what I wasn't lying about?"

I nodded; I knew he'd see that.

"I was doing thumb exercises," he said. "You know, to play the game. I figured that's what it must've been. My thumbs are rusty."

"Ok, well, this time we can play a battle game," I told him. "You must do combo moves to power up, and each one has like a different finisher move. Pick who you want to play wisely."

After a moment of silence, I turned to see him staring into space, his lips pinching together. "Is this another game you're really good at?" he asked. "And will you tell me what abilities they have before we play?"

Two very fair questions. "I have one answer to both. Play and find out."

He tickled me, digging his fingers into my sides. I wiggled around until he stopped and kissed my neck. "Can I ask another question?"

"Ok," I said in a giggle.

"What things do you like about being a little?" he asked. "And what do you like from a partner?" I felt the hesitation in his voice, it wasn't an uncomfortable pause, but almost like he was trying to phrase his words right.

"I like going to a place of happiness," I said. "Everything is simple, everything is easy, there are no responsibilities in that space. And—and I like someone who is protective, giving, and someone who can take control and make the decisions for me."

He kissed my neck again as a shiver ran through me. "Someone who can sort your heating out too?"

"That's something they might take care of."

"I guess it makes sense, those are the types of qualities

in a good Daddy, right?"

Hearing him say *Daddy* sent another thrill through me. "Exactly."

"Does it turn you on?" he asked, his hands stroking at my chest, gently across my nipples.

My voice turned quiet. "If you're good at it, it might."

"Ok," he said, giving my neck another kiss. "Now, would a Daddy lose a game on purpose, or would he try winning?"

I gasped. "Obviously, I'll win, you don't need to lose the game on purpose."

"Game on then little sassy pants," he said, tickling me again.

Fighting games were one of my favorites. I usually played one of the women with the unrealistic body proportions and could wield some type of magic. Those were the best.

Loading the game, Marcus's eyes were glued to the screen as he went through all the characters. I'd already picked mine, Yana, a woman in a red dress with two slits up either side and a diamond cutout showing her boobs. The leg slits gave her great room for kicking, and her finishing move was a giant thunder blast that looked like it came from her boobs. Marcus, typical for a guy picked the guy with the big muscles with all the veins pulsing.

"It's three rounds," I explained. "But if I win two, then I win. If you win two, then—then it's a miracle." I burst into laughter as he pretended to pounce on me.

As expected, I won. My move combos hit every single time, slamming his character into the ground, and then once he was there, I powered up and used my finisher. He was burned to a crisp.

"We can play one more game, and then I'll have to go," he said.

"No, no. Why don't you stay the night?" I asked.

I was eager. It came out of nowhere. I'd meant it, but I didn't want to move things too fast. He was nice, and we'd just had sex. All the dopamine hormones were going crazy inside me. He had every mind to say no and stick to his plan.

"Ok," he said. "But I have to be up super early."

"How early is super early?"

He chuckled. "You can't take the invite back now."

"Good. I snore," I said. "And I have a spare toothbrush, so we've got that covered."

"You snore, well, I sometimes get a boner in my sleep."

Now I wouldn't want to, especially not when I knew how my bed felt with him in it.

That night, we spent it cuddling each other, and I had Oinky in my arms. His body clung to mine almost as much as I clung to him. And I didn't want to let him go. I was so wrapped up in sleeping beside him, I wished I could've woken up more to be reminded that he was still in bed and then I could close my eyes with that same excitement. It's probably why I woke up at dawn when I felt his warmth vanish from beside me.

"Hey, sleepy," he whispered from the kitchen at the opposite end of the apartment. "Um—so, you really don't have anything in your fridge." He walked back over to me, but my eyes were fixed on the little hair poking out above his briefs.

"I—I told you, I haven't been grocery shopping," I said before turning over and shoving my face in the pillow and reaching out for Oinky.

His warmth was back with me again, his hands around my waist, his mouth kissing on my neck. "Well, we have one other option. I own a bakery, and we make breakfast pastries."

Usually, I would've been mad about waking up so early, but a surprise to my system, I was onboard with everything he was saying. "You're gonna make me breakfast?" I asked.

"I'll make you breakfast, I'll stroke your face, I'll do whatever you want me to." His soft words had my eyes fluttering to the back of my head. "I even make this delicious peppermint mocha; it's got this high-quality chocolate and these expensive coffee beans." With cadence of each word had me by the throat. My thighs squeezed together, and my toes curled. "What do you think?"

Opening my mouth, a moan came out. "Oh my god. Yes, firstly. Sounds like you just fucked my ear with dirty talk. But—but it was just food." I turned around to be face to face. "Anyway, yes, I'm ready for you to work your magic on me. I'm—oh god."

"Are you hard right now?" he asked, trying to look down. Oinky was in the way of the view. He kissed my nose. "Well, how about we get some breakfast in us first," he said. "It's the most important meal of the day."

He was so right, and I felt so taken care of. "Okay."

Pulling away, he nodded to the beanbag. "I went through and grabbed you something to wear."

I grabbed hold of his arm so tight. I couldn't explain it to him. I felt emotionally edged.

He sorted out a nice outfit. It was a red and yellow Christmas sweater, and from my grandma's neat writing on the inside label, I could tell it was from a couple years ago. A white under t-shirt, jeans, a pair of red briefs with Christmas bells on, and red socks. There was clearly a theme.

The street was surprisingly active for such an early start. Hinton was a bustling small town, and on Main Street, the same street of the accountancy office, there were many stores, including the bakery at one end of the street.

A large van was out on the road spreading salt to clear away any ice and melt the thick snow into a slurry. People stopped Marcus as we walked by them, each one striking up conversation about collection on their Christmas desserts.

"I've got about fifty desserts to make up, and I can't make them all in advance, so next week is gonna be hectic," he said, taking hold of my gloved hand in his. People saw, but nobody in town cared who you were with, they only cared that people were happy and safe.

"Maybe we should've gone to the café," I said.

Marcus scoffed. "If we did that, then I'd probably late for work."

I'd almost forgot he had to work. "I guess we also get some more alone time."

"That's what I want," he said.

Marcus let me into the bakery and turned the heating on before he left me waiting to go to his apartment upstairs for a change of clothes.

I took the time to look around the bakery. I remembered when I was younger and I had a toy kitchen. I'd pretend to make meals with wooden blocks painted as different foods. It took me back to that moment, but this time, everything was real, polished metal and chrome rather than the bright colorful pastels of my childhood play kitchen.

The fridges were stocked, several of them. He had stacks of eggs, butter, milk, and buckets filled with chocolate. I didn't touch any of it, but the temptation to dig a finger into a bucket of chocolate was strong. There were also bowls wrapped with plastic wrap. I didn't know what they were for, but I allowed myself to wonder it was for gingerbread cookies.

"Find anything interesting?" Marcus asked. "I was thinking, for breakfast I can make amazing butter croissants and fill them with chocolate, or pistachio, people always come in asking for them with pistachio spread."

Gulping with hunger. "I'm down."

"Great," he said, taking an apron from a hook. "I'm gonna have to make them anyway. You want to help?" He took a second apron. "In fact, I think I need someone with your touch."

His compliments tingled me, like someone blowing on the back of my neck.

The hard part of the croissants was already done. The part I was given was to twist the dough into the shape of a croissant with the small ends, often curled in on each other. Together, we made a batch of them. We used all the space in the stacked oven.

"You always wanted to own a bakery?" I asked.

"I've always wanted to bake," he said. "It's a lot of work, but I love it, and I love seeing people's faces when they bite into something I've made."

I wished I had a passion like that. I never knew what I'd always wanted. I'd just wanted to be happy. I suppose I'd found that happiness within my little space, and within playing games and getting cuddles. I suppose I also enjoyed numbers, figures, things that were solid. It was easy to disconnect myself from numbers, which meant once I stopped working my day job, I didn't take it home with me.

"I promised you one of my world-famous mochas too," he said.

Marcus walked around the kitchen as I sat at a counter,

staring at the ovens in hopes the croissants would bake faster.

The phone rang as he patted coffee grounds into the machine.

"Want me to get that?" I asked.

"No, no, your job is important," he said. "Keep an eye on those croissants."

As he answered the phone, the hum of the machine gargled and the deep, intense smell of coffee brewing took my attention. Marcus approached me, a strained smile on his face.

"I have a favor to ask."

"Hit me with it."

"That was Sara, she was supposed to be coming in this morning," he said. "Could you stick around a little after breakfast to help?"

I looked around with wonder. "Does that mean I become a baker for the day?"

His warm hand took mine. "A baking assistant."

"Yes, I'd love to help!" It saved me from going back to the apartment and reliving last night, which wasn't a bad thing, but if I got to make more memories with Marcus, I wasn't going to turn it down. "I don't know what my skills are, but I'm good with a cookie cutter."

After two delicious butter croissants filled with chocolate spread, and a mocha that massaged from the inside, we got to work. Watching Marcus take control was incredible. He had everything he wanted doing for the day on a whiteboard, there were so many cupcakes, cookies, and croissants, as well as a couple things I couldn't pronounce.

As the morning progressed, his other employee, Bethany arrived. She worked the counter, tending to the customers. Marcus and I rolled out a sheet of gingerbread cookie dough. He was very hands on in his approach, going gently and soft with his method.

"We have a lot of metal cutters," he said, opening a drawer filled with metal shapes. "Of course, gingerbread people, snowflakes, hearts, snow people, Christmas trees, stockings, candy canes, reindeer, and angels."

Cutting shapes from the sheet of cookie dough; I was a natural baker.

"Once they've baked, we cool them, and then we decorate," he said. "But maybe not like the other day, because you exploded a piping bag."

That moment replayed on a loop; it was the tension between us that popped the piping bag. Now, that tension was gone; we'd explored each other since then. Plus, I gave good hand—movement and pressure. I could pipe frosting all day.

SIX

MARCUS

The smell of bread and cookies in the air was heaven on the senses and seeing Leland help was the cherry on top. I felt incredibly lucky to have things work out like this, but I didn't want to be too forward with him. I didn't want to tell him all the things I wanted from him, which was spending every single night with him so I could explore what we had growing between us.

In the middle of the kitchen, taking a break from piping frosting, Leland pressed his chest against mine and hugged me. "My feet hurt. This is why I have a job where I can sit down."

"I have a question," I said, pushing his head back, my

hands through his hair. "Will you come to the Christmas fair on Saturday with me?" Today was Thursday. He could take his time to decide.

Squinting, he stared at me. "You mean, like, work the stall?"

"No, no. Like a date."

"You want to date me?" his voice turning meek.

I kissed his forehead. "I don't know what to do," I told him. I'd never done this before with another guy. I didn't know if there was a different way to do things. "We've had sex, so I was hoping we'd go on a date."

He giggled. "Does it count as a date if I want to spend all my time with you without a break."

The same intense thought and feeling was strong inside my heart. Every moment beside him was like a moment of bliss. "Me too," I whispered.

"Ok, in that case, maybe you'd want to come to the shelter with me tonight," he said. "My mom said you never go, and I'm sure people would love to see the person they have to thank for all the delicious desserts."

I didn't donate to be thanked, I donated because it was the right thing to do. I knew the shelter wasn't just for the homeless, the shelter was a place where people living on the breadline went to receive food packages and sometimes get a warm meal cooked. "Sure, and I'll make sure they know that today, you helped out."

"But it's your business, you deserve the recognition."

An oven timer sounded. "That's the chocolate sponge cake," I said, kissing his lips.

Each day, I made sure we had bread baked, all different types of bread; loaves, baguettes, and rolls. Then came the sweet stuff, cakes, small cupcakes, and cookies. Sometimes, depending on the orders, I made wedding cakes and other celebration cakes. On particularly busy days, I had two helpers in the kitchen and one out serving customers, but most of the time, I made do with Bethany and Sara.

Getting recognition for donating made me nervous. I purposefully made more food than I'd sell for the purpose of helping the community. The business was doing well financially. I owned the building outright. The main expenses came from utilities and ingredients.

"I don't think I should have another coffee," Leland said, his fingers tapping away on the metal counter. "It's so strong."

He made me chuckle, his actions were adorable, everything he did, and I didn't know if he knew what they were doing to me. "I use it mostly in food," I told him. "You have to dilute it to drink."

"But I love coffee!" he shouted. "It's so good! I feel like I could run a marathon. Or—or maybe I could polish these surfaces into mirrors." In a hyperactive whir, he grabbed a cloth and started cleaning the counters.

Maybe it wasn't the best idea to have fed him sweet treats and sugary snacks all day. This wasn't exactly where people came to for savory food needs, except for bread, everything else was a dessert. "Want me to make you a sandwich?" I asked him.

"No, no, my mom's made beef stew," he said.

I was stalling. The bakery was clean. The leftovers were bagged up. I was nervous to leave and go to the shelter.

Leland didn't notice it until he saw me standing at the exit door. I had my winter coat on, a thick beanie on my head, and my gloves. His smile only eased me a little, followed by a hug, wrapping his arms around my waist. He squeezed and I squeezed back, trying to become one.

"If you're nervous about my mom seeing us together, you don't have to be," he said.

"I'm not, I'm—just wondering how I can impress her," I told him, although partly a lie. His mom was incredibly sweet, and she came in once a week or so. In fact, she'd already placed her order for a gingerbread cheesecake. It was an incredibly popular choice of dessert. She'd told me it was Leland's favorite.

"Just be yourself," he said, clinging to me. "But we should go, and be early, she'll be impressed by that."

The shelter was near the town square and town hall. The town square was where the Christmas fair was taking place. It was a huge space with a statue of the town founder, Edmund Hinton. He was decorated in colorful twinkling lights, as were the trees and bushes. It was magical, and we walked slower to admire it. Another stalling tactic.

"Come on," Leland said. "I'm hungry."

The shelter doubled up as both a community center and food bank. It was alive with the spirit of Christmas. Decorations decked the walls; lights and tinsel.

"Mistletoe!" he shouted, yanking my arm at the decoration above the arched doorway. I looked down and kissed him.

"Aw, well isn't that a surprise," Leland's mom said, catching us. She had tight curled brown hair and wore a chunky knit Christmas sweater. She pawed a hand at the bag in mine. "Two little love birds. Is this dessert?"

Maybe this wasn't the best impression to make, kissing her son. It wasn't the first impression, since I'd known his mom for years, but to be seen kissing him like this after she'd only just mentioned him moving back.

"We're dating," Leland said before I could get a word out.

"Great," she said. "Do you want to come help me put these out?" She asked, staring into my eyes. "And Leland, can you stand at the stew station and dish it out?"

"Sure," he said, pulling away his jacket as he walked inside.

Leland's mom grinned as I stood. "Come on," she said. "You look like a deer in headlights."

I was a deer in headlights, the lights of the hall filled with people eating at tables and lining up to be served from the tables set up with food around the side of the hall.

"You know, Lisa," she said, introducing me to an older woman with gray hair. "Lisa runs this place."

"Hi, I didn't know you organized this," I said. I'd seen her around. She hadn't always had gray hair, but she'd been a vocal person in town.

"I'm glad you made it," she said. "Your help in the community hasn't gone unnoticed. We appreciate it."

"It's nothing," I said, feeling my face grow warm. I pulled away the scarf from my neck.

"Ooh, what's that?" Leland's mom asked, touching my neck. "Looks like a bruise."

The heat was getting worse in my face. I knew it was a bruise, but it was a bruise from a love bite. "Should we go inside?" I prompted. "I've heard a lot of wonderful things about your stew, Mrs. Jenkins."

She chuckled. "Oh, sweetheart, call me Cora."

"Cora," I said.

"Let me fix you up a little stew then."

"And maybe some for Leland too," I added. "He hasn't eaten much today. He was helping in the bakery, so most of what he ate was sugar."

His mom chuckled. "You know, that might be why he tried eating you," she said. "It's alright, a little concealer will cover it up."

I placed a hand over the love bite on my neck, although I knew she was joking, it was all so intense. "Things just happened," I said. "I didn't even notice this, so maybe I should make sure he's properly fed in future."

"I'm just playing," she said, leading me behind a counter with a spot reserved for the pastries I'd brought with me. "You know, Lisa should make an announcement to say you're here. I'm sure people would love to give you some form of applause for all the love you've shown the community."

"Oh no," I turned quickly, making eye contact with Lisa. "That's not something I'm here for. I love to give back to the community. I grew up here, I don't want to see this town become one of those—those—" I snapped my fingers, searching for the word. "One of those ghost towns."

Lisa sighed. "A ghost town would be accurate if we didn't have such a giving community. Plus, if everyone was selfishly looking after themselves, then that's what would happen." She raised a hand, pawing at the air. "Enough of my preaching. I'll see you around, I've got some sleeping bags to prepare for a couple that just arrived from the city."

Cora introduced me to her mom, Leland's grandma. She sat in a wheelchair with a blanket over her legs and on top of that, a wicker basket with yarn and knitting needles. "Oh, aren't you handsome," she said. "Are you Leland's boyfriend?"

"No, mom, Marcus owns a bakery down the road," Cora said. "But I think they're dating."

"Yeah, I think we're dating too."

"Well then, I'll get started on making you a sweater," she

said, picking up her knitting needles. "Turn around for me so I can size you up."

I gave a turn, trying to search for Leland in the hall. There were people everywhere, and most of them appeared to be wearing sweaters like the ones I'd seen him wearing.

"What are your folks doing for the holiday?" Cora asked as she laid out the pastries.

Locking eyes with Leland as he dished out bowls of stew, he smiled and waved.

"My folks are in Florida," I said. "They invited me down with them, but I have the bakery to run, and gingerbread cheesecakes to make."

Her eyes lit up as she smacked her lips. "Well, I'm not going to complain about that. But if you don't have plans for Christmas, then you should come and spend it with us at our home."

"That's really kind of you to offer, Mrs. Jenkins."

"I told you already, it's Cora," she said. "And I assure you, it's no problem. My other son is bringing his girlfriend, so it'll be nice that Leland has someone over as well. A full house."

Her offer filled me with the same warmth that Leland filled me with. But again, I didn't want to overstep. It gave me butterflies. I also didn't want to move too quick, I wanted this to be something that would last, and there was only one way that would last, and that's if I got to know a little more about Leland and what he wanted from me.

I took a moment to stand against the wall. I needed to do a little research.

How to be a good daddy? I searched online.

Perhaps a mistake. I didn't want parenting websites.

I could've asked Leland what he wanted, but I also wanted for some things to feel like they were coming to me intuitively.

After a couple moments, I found a site. It talked about what a Daddy and little relationship looked like. There were different levels to it, going from vanilla all the way through to hardcore. I'd probably have to ask him where he fell on that scale. There were elements to the play. Dressing up, rewards, punishments, activities of nurture, and setting rules.

'Being confident in the play as a Daddy or Mommy is important. Your little wants someone to take control.'

"What's up?" Leland's voice startled me.

"Nothing, just out of my element here," I told him.

He presented a small bowl of stew with a torn bread roll. "You looked hungry." He held a second bowl for himself.

"I'm the one who should've been taking care of you," I said, thinking about what he might've liked from me.

Leland smirked, shrugging at me. "You have all day," he said. "I just wanted to repay the favor. And my mom told me she invited you over to celebrate Christmas."

"She did."

"Are you going to?"

"Do you want me to?"

Furrowing his brows, Leland stared at me. "Do you want to?"

"Absolutely I do," I said, taking the spoon from his bowl with some stew on it. "Also, your mom spotted that love bite." I spooned the food into Leland's mouth. His eyes lit up, almost on the verge of euphoric tears. "You like being fed?"

"Yes, Daddy."

SEVEN

I'd only had one previous partner who I was involved with as a little and he took care of me as a Daddy. It wasn't for everyone. I enjoyed the more vanilla side of the play, which was feeding, playing, and giving me the place to go into little space. For Marcus, I knew it was new. I was the first guy he'd slept with, and now I was introducing him to a kink that should've scared him off.

I invited him to stay over again while we were at the shelter. He agreed immediately. He couldn't leave fast enough. He said it wasn't because he didn't want to stay, but because he wanted to grab a couple things to bring over.

"He's a nice boy," Mom said as she saw me putting my

coat on and wrapping up in my scarf. "But I want to make sure you're eating. I saw that mark you left on his neck."

"Mom." I froze, looking around, nobody except my grandma was even paying attention.

Grandma was busy knitting and giggling to herself.

"Will I see you tomorrow?" Mom asked. "I need some help preparing for the fair on Saturday. I'm making several stews, and I need help with the veggies."

"Yes, I'll be over," I told her. "I still need to head to the mall to get you something for Christmas as well."

She cooed. "Nothing too fancy," she said. "It's open late tomorrow night, the last Friday before Christmas."

I gave them both hugs before leaving. I enjoyed helping at the shelter when I could, it reminded me how good I'd had things growing up and even now. Some people even came to town to get help, and we were always willing to get people on their feet. That's what made the town magical.

Marcus was outside my apartment, a big smile on his pinched pink face. "We have to stop meeting like this," he said.

He was right; I could barely keep my footing on this snowy sidewalk. In the city, the air had a high salt content or something because the snow never stuck as well as it did here.

"We really do," I called back to him.

He kissed me as soon as I was close enough. "I'm sorry about back there," he said.

"I get it," I said. "You're a strong, silent type. Now, Mr. Strong-Silent, I want to get upstairs and into something more comfortable."

"As long as I can get into *someone* more comfortable." Marcus wiggled his brows. "I also brought supplies. Hot chocolate, whipped cream, some coconut oil, you know, essentials." He raised his bag, grinning down at me.

Inside the apartment, whatever Marcus had done to it yesterday had fixed the major issues. It was warm, almost too warm, but I wasn't about to complain and have the entire heating system shut down and leave us cold— although maybe an opportunity to cuddle.

I caught Marcus watching me as I dug into the box of onesies. "You want to choose the one I wear?"

"Sure." He smiled. "I was wondering what other things you'd like me to do. You know, I want to explore it a little more with you. And I kinda searched online."

"Oh no." I knew the perils of searching the internet for things like this. "And what did you find?"

Marcus let out a puff of air, inflating his cheeks. "Some very hardcore stuff."

I placed a hand a chest, feeling the thud of his heartbeat. "Well, I'm not really into anything hardcore, I just—I like the caring aspect. And when I feel cared for, I might get a little—naughty, or playful, excited, you know."

"Horny," he said, after I skirted around the word.

"Yes," I giggled.

He placed his hand over mine. "You know I've always sorta cared for you," he said. "You knew about my secret before it was a secret, you—you were the only guy I wanted to kiss. And you still are."

Kissing, we bridged the gap of our bodies. My fingers clawing into his sweater, wishing I had the ability to tear it off him.

"I want to tell you the truth," I said.

"Ok."

"When you kissed me that first time during the New Year's party, I thought that was because you knew I was gay, and you thought it was funny to just kiss me because it was midnight." I let it out. It was something I'd held in for a while, not in a tormented type of way, but in a reflective wanting, and a source of many boners. "The second time, I figured, maybe you lost a bet, again. The third time was different. The third time you kissed me, there was something in you that took over and—"

Again, our lips locked. His hand at the back of my head, cradling it in place as he took control of caressing me. Each time he kissed me, it was like those same firework explosions from New Year's Eve. The belltower ringing out with its loud tolls and Marcus's tongue a mixture between beer and peppermint.

Pausing, and out of breath, he stared in my eyes. "You like it when I call you a good boy?"

"I am a good boy," I whispered.

"Today, at the bakery, you were a very good boy."

I went in to kiss his neck and realized that was where I'd left the love bite.

"Maybe you want to try to leave your mark below the neck this time," he said, slipping his fingers up my sweater. "I'd like to leave a mark on yours."

Once he made a move with his hands, I knew I was free to make my move. I wanted him undressed completely, more because I wanted to see it when guys were naked, because their clothes were protection, and it was like looking behind their protection. To see them completely raw was electricity in my veins.

"Hold on," he said, clenching his belt buckle to keep me going further. "I have something I want to do to you."

"You do?"

"Do you like massages?"

I gasped. "I love them. Will you massage me?"

"That's what I was planning on doing." He pecked my nose with a quick kiss. "I have coconut oil. But I want to warn you, after a massage, you might fall in love with me."

"Might," I said, my voice breaking.

I didn't know if I was already there. I'd thought about Marcus and moments like these since that very first kiss. It was the dream that I would catch a jock's eye and he'd whisk me away to homecoming. Maybe that was because I grew up watching a lot of the same movies. Those thoughts and feelings were there, almost implanted in me, both very real and very sudden.

"You want to go get ready?" he asked. "Get undressed, lay on the bed with your head on your pillow. I'll warm the coconut oil."

"You sound like a professional."

Leaning in, his mouth to my ear. "I don't think a professional would be getting naked and using his body to massage your body, do you?"

Stuck for words, I shook my head. I was ready for his magical hands to rub all over me. I was already boned up and tucked to the right of my underwear without the massage.

Undressing, I watched Marcus place a small glass jar of coconut oil in the microwave. He watched me right back, licking his lips, his eyes looking up and down, slowly, as if taking thousands of pictures.

I turned around before taking off my underwear, so that all he saw was my bum.

"Perfection," he said.

Laying front down on my bed, I inhaled his scent from where he'd slept last night. "Will this make a mess?" I asked. "The oil, I mean."

"Oh, actually, it might leave oil marks, you want to do it on a towel?"

I shook my head. "Oh no, it will give me a reason to go buy new sheets." My mind already giddy from the excitement of knowing that his hands were about to be all over me, but now, mixed in with the thought that I was going to buy new bedding.

My boner rubbed against the bedding, anticipation and excitement brewing inside me about him, I was ready and waiting. Listening for his footsteps growing closer to me.

"It's going to be warm," he said. Turning slightly, he tutted at me. "Head down," he instructed. "I hope you're ready for me to treat your body with the care and attention it deserves."

Well, he had told me earlier I was a good boy, so it made perfect sense for him to be rewarding me now.

The wave of warm relaxation rolled over my body with his hands, first at the base of my back, just above my bum. A pooling warmth tingled on my skin just as his fingers began gliding up my back. I let out a deep moan, almost as if it had been exorcised out of me. He stretched up along my body, reaching my shoulders, spreading the warm oil.

"You like that, baby?" he asked, pushing his face to my ear, resting his chin on my shoulder.

"Yes, Daddy," I whispered. "Do I have any tension in my back?"

His chest pressed harder against my back, resting on me. A gentle click popped in my back as I relaxed deeper onto the mattress.

His fingers were magic, and I was usually ticklish, but I was exhilarated to feel his fingers rolling up and down my sides. My eyes rolled back with the high level of relaxation I was in. I didn't even realize his throbbing cock was there, pressing at my lower back.

"That feels good," I said, pushing out a shallow breath.

He pulled away and poured more of the warm oil. It coated me, spread down with his fingers, all the way to my bum. He squeezed, massaging and clenching as he pulled my cheeks apart to see my hole. More warm oil touched my skin, going between my cheeks and covering my puckered tight hole.

"What about this?" he asked, inserting just a fingertip to tease me.

I was more than pleased about that. "Yes, I like that."

"Good boy." He slipped in a second finger, unless my hole had become loose and that was in fact a third finger, or worse an entire fist. I knew how lubricating coconut oil was. I tried clenching around his finger, but it seemed useless. He was more than able to insert and pull his finger out at will.

Imagining myself as a piece of dough in his bakery as he worked his knuckles and fingers into my back, I thought I would melt like butter into my sheets. "Fuck me," I whispered. "Hard."

I turned my head to see him throw a torn condom wrapper across the bed. "No peeking," he said as I felt his thick-headed cock press against my hole. He went in, all lubed. His hips pressing against my ass. I gasped, my toes curling, and my legs trying to wrestle his legs. With him inside me, I didn't know if it was possible to be any more than one with him, but I wanted it.

"Is it weird that I just want to lay on top of you?" he asked, massaging his thumbs up my back before laying against me again. "With my dick inside and just exist."

"I—I want that," I said, gulping on the raw emotion bubbling in my throat.

Backing up, as if I could take more of him inside me. He wrapped his hands around me, slowly fucking me with his hard thrusts.

I didn't know if it was possible to feel the way he was making me feel. Our history together came to a point, like the apex of a mountain we'd both climbed together, and now we were enjoying the view. It was breathtaking, and our limbs fell into each other.

Turning me over on my back to massage my chest with his cock still inside me, I was on the verge of cumming.

Seeing him kneeling on the bed, spreading my legs, I fought every urge in me to shoot my load.

His warm lubed hand grabbed my cock. "Cum for me baby."

It was the only command I needed. Only a couple pumps of his hand along my shaft and I came up my chest, my cum mixing in with the coconut oil. I felt him slowly pull out as my hole was clenching.

Leaning forward, I took his cock to jerk it and he came, shooting his load on the lower half of my face.

"Baby, I'm sorry, I—"

Extending my tongue, I licked it. "It was a nice surprise." And my first real taste of him, the product he'd made pumping inside me, now on my face like a glorious reward.

Cleaning my face with his t-shirt from the side of the bed, he leaned in a kissed my forehead.

He laid beside me, our legs entangled and our arms holding each other.

"Smells like a bakery in here," he said.

"Mmm, now I'm hungry." I smacked my lips. "Did you bring any cookies with you?"

"I suppose you've already had my cream, so it's only natural you want cookies too."

I giggled. He tickled me. It turned to wrestling.

Everything felt right. I didn't want to leave his space. And I hoped he felt the same about me.

EIGHT

MARCUS

I couldn't get Leland out of my head, and he wasn't going to be at work with me at all tomorrow. His mom needed him for some help, although I knew I couldn't keep him around me for another day. I feared he might've started to get sick of me.

Today was a busy day in the bakery, I had a lot to prepare for the Christmas fair tomorrow.

Sara sauntered into the kitchen of the bakery, stuffing her red hair inside a net. "I heard you got your new boyfriend to come in and help you yesterday."

Pouring cake batter into tins, I was too focused to pay attention.

"I saw Marcia the other day," she said. "Does she know?"

She finally had my attention. "I only dated Marcia for a couple months, three years ago," I chuckled. "Didn't she get married like a year ago?"

Sara shrugged. "Oh, I thought it was a recent thing. I knew you were bi; you did that whole pastry thing for bisexual visibility day."

"And Leland isn't my boyfriend," I told her. "Leland is someone I'm seeing."

"He's cute," she sighed. "Also, I'm sorry I couldn't come in yesterday. I don't know what happened."

"I do," I remarked. "Bethany mentioned she saw you slinging back shots at *Ziggy's.*"

Sara gasped. "It's Christmas, I was taken by the Christmas spirit—or spirits, vodka, gin, you name it."

"Well, you're here now. Look at the board, we have a lot of work to do today."

She gave me a salute before turning to view the whiteboard.

Baking distracted me from my evening with Leland, because every time I went to think about it, I became aroused and that was incredibly unsanitary to be doing in here. At least, it was while I was working. After hours, alone with Leland, I might've felt differently.

The kitchen seemed to be doused with gingerbread spices. We were in the midst of making gingerbread men and gingerbread houses, most of it for display tomorrow at the fair.

I didn't even realize what time it was until the back door of the bakery opened and Leland walked inside, shaking off the snow in the doorway.

"Oh, hello," Sara said, taking a moment from gluing the gingerbread house together with frosting.

He stared at me, grinning. "Hi."

"I had an entire thing planned for when you came," I said, pushing the cooling rack of cookies on the shelf.

"Should I leave for this?" Sara asked, looking from him and back to me.

"It's fine," I said, approaching Leland. "I didn't realize how late it got. So, since tonight is the last late shopping night at the mall, I was wondering if you'd want to come with me."

He giggled, brushing away snow from his face with his gloved hand. "You know, I was actually going to ask you the same thing. I've got to get my folks gifts, plus, I want to see Santa."

I closed the space between our bodies. "You want to see Santa?" I asked in a whisper. "To sit on his lap?"

"I don't think I'd like to sit on a stranger's lap," he said. "But if you have a lap free, then I'll be happy enough to sit on it and tell you all the things I want for Christmas."

"And—" my breathing grew deep and intense. "Since you've been a good boy, I'm sure that you'll get whatever it is you ask for."

He butted down his lips, creating little dimples in his rosy cheeks. "Can I tell you what I want now?" he whispered. "Or do we have to wait until I'm on your lap?"

"Now you're being naughty," I said, my chest heavy, trying to control myself. "Let me finish up here, and we can go to the mall."

Giggling, he nodded. "Should I meet you back here, or do you want to meet me outside the shelter?"

"I can't ask you to walk all the way to the shelter and back," I said, a smile burning my cheeks. "Plus, I'm driving, so I'll pick you up in about thirty minutes." I took a look around to see Sara focused. I gave Leland a kiss.

After the kiss, he paused, his eyes still closed. "Would it be weird to say I missed you today?" he asked quietly.

"I've actually missed you too," I said, kissing him again. "Ok, donations. If you go through to the front, Bethany has them. The kitchen already has too much going on."

After each heated encounter that made me feel like I'd been in a relationship with Leland for years, I had to remind myself about how new all of this was. I didn't want to move at a fast pace, but then with of those thoughts, I was reminded that this has been years in the making. Each one of those kisses had created something between us.

Everything at the bakery was prepared for tomorrow. I'd have to come in early to finish some things off, but the Christmas fair was going to be great, not because of the pastries and cookies, but because I was going to be there with Leland and holding his hand. Sara had seen us kissing, and tomorrow people would see us holding hands, it was no big deal. But it was also a huge deal.

I drove a red Prius. Leland had been standing in the doorway of the shelter, staring up at the sky when I pulled up to collect him. He was staring at the snowfall as it caught the light from the nearby lamp. He looked at it with wonder I envied about him.

"Ok, I have a list," he said, pulling his gloves off and warming his hands up on the heated vents. "My mom is obsessed with tea pots and weird teas, the ones nobody can pronounce with flowers that sounds like poison. My dad will just get some scotch. I need to grab grandma some yarn, apparently there's a sale in the fabric store. And my brother will have to make do with a pack of condoms, apparently, he has this new girlfriend, and I don't think I'm old enough to be called an uncle just yet."

I couldn't stop watching his lips as he told me his list. It was a good job I'd parked to pick him up, otherwise I'd be considered incredibly dangerous. "And don't forget you wanted to sit on Santa's lap," I snickered.

He pawed a hand at my lap, gently tapping. "That's not—completely accurate," he said. "Are you jealous?"

A little. "No."

"You can tell me if you are, I'd be jealous if someone wanted to sit on your lap," he said, his voice growing quiet.

I leaned over and kissed him. "Don't worry, I'm sure if my lap was free to be sat on, I'd only want you there," I told him, not realizing just how gushy what I'd said was. "We should go though, I have somewhere I wanted to take you."

"We," he scoffed. "You're the one in the driver's seat."

Usually, so cool, calm, and collected, I didn't know how Leland had such control over me. I felt like I was losing brain power, since the blood could only flow and pump so hard. Most of the blood was in my dick, naturally.

The Hinton Mall was huge. It was what Hinton was most known for, a small town with a big mall. I rarely made it out here, only when I needed new clothes, or a trip to the cinema, but I worked all the time. The last film I saw in the cinema was one with Zac Efron in it. It might've also been around the time of a bisexual awakening. Even now, I'd sacrifice my left nut for a taste of Zac's Efron. His penis, that was his Efron.

Most of the town was at the mall tonight. It was the last late night of Christmas shopping. I hadn't shopped much, my family were away, but I'd sent them gift cards. It helped pay my folks apps. My mom had been playing this one matching game, and she sank hundreds of dollars into it for powerups. It brought her joy and happiness, so I knew what to get her for the holidays.

It was nice to walk through the mall, holding Leland's hand. At first, he asked me if I was sure. His big, deep green eyes staring at me, concerned that I wasn't out about my sexuality. I didn't want him to care about any of that, it wasn't anyone else's business but ours. I kept tight hold of his hand.

"I always forget how hard this town goes for the holidays," Leland said, his head on a swivel as everything in the mall was vying for his attention. Lights, tinsels, and the artificial intense scent of Christmas was everywhere. Cinnamons and other spices caught in the tip of my nose.

"Look, there's Santa." In the center of the mall, children queued up to sit on Santa's lap. A man in a white beard and red Santa suit with white stuffing peeping out. "You still want to sit on his lap?" I whispered, tugging him closer.

"Noooo," he said, playfully attacking me with a hand at my chest. "Your lap is the only one I want to sit on. Plus, I know he's not the real Santa."

Staring into his eyes, still, he was the only person in the world to me. "So, you don't want to?" I pressed my lips against his, a long pause as we connected.

Leland gasped, pulling away, like he'd held his breath for the duration we'd kissed. "You're more like Santa," he whispered. "You've actually helped me tick things off my wishlist."

This was new. He hadn't mentioned a wishlist. "What else is on your wishlist?"

Realizing we were surrounded by hundreds of other people; we stepped closer to a window display out of the path of foot traffic.

"If I tell you what's on my wishlist, then it might not all come true," he said.

I respected that, but he already gave me ideas about what was on that wishlist by telling me I'd helped him tick things off it.

"Wasn't that guy someone from our high school?" he said, seemingly distracting me. He gestured to the elf standing beside Santa.

"Kamden," I said. I recognized his face, although he didn't have a facial hair in high school. "He was a couple years below me."

Leland let out a giddy squeal, tapping at my arm. "Have you seen the way he's looking at the Santa? I bet they're boning."

"Is he gay?"

"Duh," he chuckled. "I thought he'd make it big as an actor or something, he was always in the school plays." He sighed. "I think it's for the best that people didn't leave Hinton. I lowkey wish I never left."

"You think if you never left, something would've happened between us?"

It wasn't something I wanted to think about, but I tortured myself with it anyway, because I loved to think about what would've happened all the time. Like, wondering what would've happened if I never came out as bisexual, and what would've happened if I stayed with my ex. I could've been married and with a child.

"I think it would," he said, pulling me out of thought as I looked around at the couples with their children as they queued to meet Santa and his elf. "You know I fancied you in high school."

"I think where we've been and what we've done in life has led us all the way up to this moment," I told him. "Being together."

"Together," he giggled. "Sounds like you're asking me to be something more than dating."

I tickled a finger under his chin. "I asked you to the mall because I wanted to take you some place."

It was something Bethany had mentioned to me, she'd bought her nephew a teddy from the *Teddy Plaza*, a popular store in the mall, filled with all different stuffed teddies on offer. But there was one that caught my eye when I was surfing their website in anticipation for inviting Leland.

"Where are we going?" he asked as I led him to the second floor of the mall.

With an arch of balloons and bright yellow branding, the magical teddy store.

"Ta-da!" I said, gesturing it to him. "They have this—" Before I could finish my sentence, Leland raced on ahead into the store.

Leland went right to the teddy I'd been eying up online. "It's a pig!" he said, his eyelids snapping wide open. "It's so squishy!" He wrapped his arms around it, squeezing it tight, close to his chest.

"And there's clothes for it too," I said. "It's what I brought you here for."

"But I already have Oinky," he whispered. "I can't replace him."

"No, no, no, not replace him. Oinky should have a friend," I said. "A Christmas present, from me."

He turned around, growing silent as he looked at the shelves of clothes for the stuffed pig teddy.

"What are you thinking?" I asked, placing a hand on his shoulder.

Leland sighed. "I don't know what to get you now."

I hugged him from behind, not caring about anyone who saw. "I thought I was Daddy," I said. "And you're my good boy. It's my responsibility to reward you. I know you'll reward me later with hugs and kisses. And I want you to spend the night at my place."

"But all my things are at mine," he said.

"All your things are still in boxes," I told him. "We can grab some things, but I want to share my space with you as well. Plus, I know you're curious about it."

"Ok, but I'll need to get my onesie, Oinky, and my toothbrush," he said.

That was an easy deal.

NINE

LELAND

Marcus's apartment was small, but it was cozy. It was filled with all of his things, from a wall of certificates to a cabinet of trophies, and covered behind a pane of glass, there was a cabinet filled with snow globes. It smelled just like the bakery below, and it was toasty warm. I'd managed to drop gifts off at my apartment and grab supplies before we came over.

I was nervous to be away from my things, but those nerves disappeared around Marcus. He relaxed me with just a look, and I was weak at the knees, ready for him to pleasure me with his magic candy cane cock. And now, it was going to look like a candy cane because he bought some red and white striped condoms.

"This is it," he said. "I don't really have guests over, so I hope it doesn't disappoint you."

"It's not the size of the room, it's what you can do in it," I said, nodding as I mashed up whatever the saying was.

Marcus grinned. He sat in the large armchair, kicking off his boots. "Why don't you come over here and I'll show you what I can do." He spread his legs and pushed a hand into the front of his trousers. "Come sit on Daddy's lap."

Salivating with anticipation, I tried pulling my pants off and tripped over. Luckily, I fell straight into his lap.

"That's one way to go about it," he said, stroking a hand down the side of my face. "Are you going to tell me what you want for Christmas?"

Adjusting myself, I sat on his lap, leaning into his chest and listened to the quiet thump of his heart beating. "All I really wanted for Christmas was to be happy," I said, admitting it to myself and him.

The city had been a source of that happiness, but it was so short lived, and it felt like I was constantly searching for something to make me happy. I knew the only place I'd ever felt the bliss and happiness of life was here, in Hinton. There was a draw to this place, like a magnet, and it pulled me.

"Are you happy now?" he asked, stroking a hand through my hair.

"Very."

He kissed my head and as he did, I felt the boner inside

his trousers move, almost like it was begging for my attention.

"Are you happy?"

"I have a gorgeous guy on my lap, a date for the Christmas fair, and plans for Christmas day, of course I am," he told me.

In my little space, I was always searching for rewards to myself, but I'd never really had a Daddy who would or could reward me. And as his cuddles put me into my little space, I couldn't help feeling like I was ready to reward him.

"Oh, what are you doing?" he asked as I got on my knees in front of him.

His trousers were already unzipped and unbuttoned, but his cock was still confined inside the prison of his underwear. "Release the beast!" I said, yanking on his underwear. His cock sprung up, standing attention. "Can I touch it?"

He chewed on his lip, both hands behind the back of his head as he grew comfortable in his armchair. "It's your toy to play with."

I would've been sad if he'd said *no*, but he didn't, and he was right. My toy.

Wasting no time, I placed my mouth around the head of his cock, my mouth stretching wide to fit the thickness inside. It was like trying to put your entire mouth over the thickest part of an ice cream cone, and it was just as tasty. Surprisingly, actually, it made me hungry to keep sucking, slurping, and tasting from tip to balls.

"Tastes so good!"

"You like that?" he asked. "It's a gingerbread body wash."

My two favorite things now together. Dick and gingerbread. My mouth didn't know whether to keep sucking or if I could get my teeth involved. Of course, I pulled away when my mind turned to teeth.

"You're a little playful, aren't ya?" he placed his hand under my chin and wiped the drool from my mouth. "I don't know if it's me, or you, or the Christmas spirit, but I'm so fucking horny for you, all the time."

I stood, toying with my trousers as I turned around and pulled them down just a little to reveal my bum. I turned my head, watching his eyes grow wider and his tongue against his lips. "What are you waiting for?" I asked. "You have my permission."

In a sweeping movement, he stood, wrapping his arms around my legs and lifting me, almost reaching the ceiling. Like flying, I let out an excited giggle and outstretched my arms to become the plane.

"And a soft landing," he said, dropping me on the bed.

His bed, which hadn't been slept in since I'd kept him with me, had a thick comforter and several fluffy blankets. It was like being hugged and tickled by thousands of small fingers, all at the same time. I wiggled around, burrowing myself into the sheet. As I moved around, he took my clothes from my body. I didn't even realize until I looked down to see my naked body.

"Your turn," I told him.

One step ahead, he was already pulling his clothes away, showing off his gorgeous tattoos and hairy chest. "I feel like a teen," he said, jumping into the bed beside me. "You bring something out of me. And I want to put it in you." He kissed my neck, his kisses turning to sucking as he went to give me a love bite.

Rolling over with him, I sat on his abdomen. Both my hands grabbed at his hairy pecs, squeezing them with excitement. He reached out and did the same back to me, but gently, he squeezed and rubbed his fingers across my nipples. It made my dick bounce, gently slapping down on his chest.

"Fuck me," I said, bouncing with the motion of the mattress on his chest. "Don't tease me, Daddy."

"Daddy doesn't tease," he whispered. "I'm just making sure you really want it."

"I do, I do!" I pound on his chest. "I really want it!"

He wrestled me, rolling us over together. "Ok, I believe you." He nestled his head into my neck and kissed. "Stay right there. I'm going to get the condoms."

I was waiting for the condoms to come out, those red and white striped condoms looking like candy canes. My hole clenched, puckering with excitement. He got them out and I volunteered to put it on him, mostly so I could touch his cock a little more. It really did look like a candy cane, but without the hook. It probably would've looked very strange if there was a hook in his cock.

"On your back again, like a good boy," he said, running a finger down my face and over my lips.

On my back, he lifted my legs up, pushing my knees to my chest and revealing my ass. He grabbed at something from the bag he'd pulled the condoms from. I tried to see, but I was sinking into the comforter. "What is it?"

"Just some lube," he said. "Gingerbread flavored. Let me know if it tingles."

The cool, tingle of the lube touched my hole. My toes curled, and my body wormed left to right. "Stop teasing me. I've been a good boy, please."

With the tip of his cock, he pressed it against my hole. With the lube, it didn't need much pressing to get it inside. The push and pulse of his body as it landed against my ass. We connected in a way I hadn't felt my body connect to another body. We rolled over, getting closer to the edge of the bed.

Sitting on his cock, I was put in control of the rhythm, each rhythmic back and forth of his cock inside me. He propped his knees up, forcing me down on his chest. My lips against his skin, looking at the faint purple-pink mark from where I'd left a love bite before, I was giving him another.

He forced my head down, my mouth and tongue on his

nipple.

Wrapping his arms around me, he kept me tight against his body before filling the condom inside me up with cum. I continued to tickle my tongue across his nipple, feeling as his cock twitched and throbbed inside me. He became ticklish, normal for post-nut pleasure.

"Cum for me now," he said, pushing my body up. He grabbed my cock, jerking it while I continued to sit on his hard cock.

Staring at him, smiling, and telling me to cum, it didn't take long. I shot my load and hit his face.

He extended his tongue out and licked the cum he could each. "Well, now I'm starving."

My stomach let out a grumble. "Oopsie." I climbed off his cock as he placed his hand on my belly, feeling for another rumble.

"What do you want to eat?"

I didn't think *you* was going to be an answer that would fill me up. He was delicious, but I needed something in me that I could chew and swallow.

After we cleaned ourselves up, he dressed me in my onesie. It was a reindeer onesie with soft, plush antlers on the hood. Marcus walked around in a pair of fleecy pajamas bottoms and a tight, white tank top. He was in his element making pasta and his own sauce simmering in a pan. I blasted Mariah Carey, it was Christmas, after all.

"You're gonna love this," he said. "It's mac and cheese,

but way better."

"Better than box mac and cheese?" I asked, taking a pause from dancing around. "Because box mac and cheese is so good and so easy to make."

He stopped stirring the pot of cheese sauce and stared at me, his mouth agape. "I'm guessing you've never dated someone who can actually cook then."

"Wow, that's so true. Usually, I've only dated guys who were good in bed and couldn't cook."

"So, I can cook, but—does that mean I'm bad in bed?"

"No, no, no, I didn't say that." I slapped my hands to my face, hiding away. "You were putting words in my mouth."

He was joking, obviously, he wasn't bad in bed. "I wish I was putting something else in your mouth."

Peering at him between my fingers, I could've gone either way, food, or more dick.

"I'm talking about the food," he said, chuckling to himself. "And it's almost ready. You want to get the table set up."

He had a small circle table with two foldable wooden chairs. I set the table with two bowls and cutlery for the both of us. Except, mine were pink, plastic, and covered in cartoon piggies. "Look," I said. "I did a good job."

"You did," he said. "A very good job from a very good boy. And you brought your favorite bowl too."

Inside, I was squealing. How did he know this was my

favorite?

I took a seat, ready and waiting. It was his food, so I was obviously going to enjoy it.

"Ok," he said, setting the pan with the macaroni noodles and sauce mixed between the bowls. "So, we should talk about what we're going to tell people tomorrow."

"I'll tell them I couldn't resist your charms, and—"

He reached out and held my hand. "I want to tell people we're dating."

"And I'll tell them I was caught spying on you from outside the bakery," I said, it was true, mostly.

"Better you spy on me than me waiting to catch you on the street," he said. "Right, let's dig in and eat." He ladled out the food into our bowls.

"But just so we're on the same page, you kissed me first at those New Year's Eve parties," I said, showing him a wide smile. I never made the first move, ever. I didn't have that level of confidence. It's why I was a little, and he was a Daddy—or at least a Daddy in training.

TEN

MARCUS

The following morning, after forcing myself to pull away from Leland in bed, I took a shower. My body tingled as if it was memory foam, and with the water washing over my body, it brought back the place where Leland's mouth and hands had been. I washed myself with the same spiced gingerbread body wash. I knew it was his favorite to smell and to taste, and I wanted him to associate those with me, that same level of wanting.

He was already rousing when I got back to the bedroom, shuffling around in the bed and letting out big stretches. It was 5 A.M. and completely dark outside. I didn't want to wake him for at least another hour. As soon as the smell of coffee brewing and the mechanical chug of the machine came alive, that plan went completely out the window.

Leland took a shower while I insisted on making breakfast and he insisted again on helping me set up for the Christmas fair.

Pancakes were on the menu for the morning. Thick, fluffy pancakes with honey from a bottle shaped like a bear. I had banana on top of mine, and he had sliced strawberries. He hadn't brought a change of clothes with him, so he climbed back into his reindeer onesie.

"You know, maybe you should wear that for the day," I suggested, watching him tear through the pancake stack with his adorable plastic piggie spork.

"I'd freeze," he said, shuddering at the idea. "Besides, if I wore this, they might think I was taking part in the town hall production, and I'm definitely not doing that."

"Jerry from the town hall actually came by the bakery to see if I wanted to be in that," I said. "I don't know what he wanted me to be, or do, but I turned him down."

"They asked my dad to be Santa."

Almost spitting a mouthful of pancakes out, I pressed a hand to my mouth.

"He said *no*, but I think it would've been so funny if he took the job. I wish he had. It would've thrown him way out of his comfort zone," he said.

Leland's dad handled my books, so I knew just the type of guy he was. He was quiet, and what you would expect from an accountant. The office was immaculate too, but also plain in a black and white chrome type of way.

The Christmas fair was one of my favorite events of the entire year. New Year's Eve was my actual favorite since that's when I really explored myself and that's when I made the first move and kissed Leland. So, of course, it required a hall of fame moment in my mind. The town was also big on celebrating the Fourth of July too. And then throughout the year, there would be smaller events that took place, and a lot of it drove business to me.

My stand was already complete, it was made of metal with a sheet on the back and a roof to protect me and whoever else was tending it. Everything I'd done yesterday was in preparation for today. The gingerbread nativity scene was what we'd been building in the bakery. It wasn't for snacking on, it was mostly for show, until the end of the evening when people would inevitably touch it, break pieces off, and all-around demolish it.

Bethany and Sara were both waiting for me outside the bakery to transport goods over. The bakery wasn't open today, so there was no fresh bread or pastries coming out of the ovens. Everything going out was what had been made yesterday. And I was relieved. It was going to be the first full day I'd have with Leland, and I wasn't trying to put too much pressure on it either.

"Is your boyfriend not joining?" Sara teased.

"He's not my—" I stopped myself. "He stayed the night,

but he's just gone home to change. He'll be over to help soon."

"At least someone is getting laid," Bethany grumbled. "What do I have to do to get some dick around here?"

Sara scoffed. "If you're lucky, Santa might drop something with a strong vibration in your stocking."

"I hope you're not kidding. The battery just died and—
"

"Ladies," I interrupted them. "The sooner we get everything out, the sooner you two can talk about sex toys together."

They giggled. "Relax, Marcus," Sara said. "I hope our talking about sex toys isn't making you uncomfortable."

"Far from it," I told them. "You said it yourself, I'm getting laid. I don't need sex toys." And with that, they only seemed to get louder in the conversation about sex toys. It didn't bother me one bit, I was listening in. There was a lot about vibrational speeds and pulsation patterns, but I didn't think my dick could do much vibrating, although around Leland, there was a pulse pattern forming, like an irregular heartbeat.

In the middle of the town square, people were setting up for the day. Sara was behind the stand, carefully organizing the gingerbread nativity scene. Bethany was trying to figure out the portable heater. And I was staring into Leland's sea glass green eyes, wondering how my Christmas wish had come true.

"My mom's over there," he whispered. "I hope she doesn't rope me into helping her with the stew." We turned to face his mom as she waved at us. "Oh no, what does she want?" he grumbled, grabbing a hold of my hand.

"I'm sure it's fine, and if she needs help, I'll volunteer to help," I told him, keeping hold of his hand.

His mom was super sweet, she always had been.

"Glued to the hip," she chuckled. "I do hope you've both been staying fed. I don't know how those marks will look when I take pictures later."

"Pictures," Leland almost choked, grabbing a tighter hold of my hand. "I—mom, this—me and—we—"

"I think pictures would be cute," I said, trying my best to calm him. As for the love bites, we were both wearing scarves, so the likelihood she'd see any of those marks were slim.

"Thank you again for those bread rolls," she said. "And if you're all set up, would you mind helping me?"

I looked deep into Leland's eyes before agreeing to it. All she wanted was for someone to fix the metal bars into the slots, and then to connect the power outlet to her heater and large slow cooker of stew.

"Your dad's coming down soon with grandma," she said, pulling Leland aside. "I might need you to keep an eye on her to make sure she doesn't go wandering. You know how she gets; she thinks she's an athlete, but in this weather, I'm worried she'd fall into the snow, and we wouldn't find her until the snow melted." She huffed and sighed, shaking her head. "I won't let it get in the way of you two canoodling."

"Maybe we should put a bell on her," Leland added with a shrug. "I mean, surely, that would be best, wouldn't it?"

She immediately let out a deep chuckle. "Your father said the same thing. She'd probably love it, actually."

Seeing how Leland was with his family made me miss mine. They knew I was going to be busy, and I knew they were content doing their own thing. It wasn't the first Christmas I'd spent without seeing my family, but it didn't mean I wasn't jealous of Leland and his.

"You two be good," Leland's mom said, shooing us away.

As the morning progressed, the decorative lights came alive, flashing with color. People slowly made their way into the town and explored all the delights. There were still stations yet to be set up, like the mulled wine, which I had my eye on as soon as they were ready. But for now, we made do with hot chocolate. It was topped with marshmallows, whipped cream, and cocoa powder.

Walking side by side around the town, Leland had one arm hooked around mine, keeping himself stable as he did his best to drink hot chocolate with his other hand. He made an adorable mess with the cream on his nose and upper lip. "This is always my favorite part of coming home for the holidays."

"I thought I was your favorite part," I said, wiping away the cream from his face.

"You—you were my favorite part of the New Year," he said. "Which actually brings me to a question. Are you going to surprise kiss me again this year? Or will it be planned."

"They weren't surprise kisses," I said. "Ok, fine, they were surprise kisses, but also, semi-drunk ones too. From both of us. And—if I remember rightly, and I do, because I thought about it for months. The second year, it felt like you didn't want to stop kissing me."

He chuckled. "I didn't want to stop kissing you, so you're right."

"Ok," I said, kissing his nose and licking the cream away. "I think they've set up the Christmas hoop toss. You want me to see if I can win you a plushie."

Leland's eye lit up. "But you just bought me one."

"And now I'm planning on winning you one."

Together, we queued up for the game. Right in front of us, my ex-girlfriend, from many years ago, stood in line.

"Marcus," she said, turning to me with her stroller. "Look at you. I saw you yesterday. So, this is a thing?"

"Hi," Leland introduced himself.

"Marcia," she said. "And this little bundle of fun is Benny. He's quiet right now. His dad's just gone off to get him some cotton candy. I don't know why though, because he'll hit a sugar high and scream down the town."

I'd seen her last night at the mall with her kid and

husband. "He's adorable."

"Are you two like a thing then?" she asked.

Leland took hold of my hand, raising it to show her.

"We're dating," I said.

She cooed. "From what I've heard, that's the most anyone has been with you in years."

She was right. I hadn't dated in years. "You know, I've got the bakery, it's busy all the time. Your mom ordered two Christmas cheesecakes from me this year." I cuddled closer to Leland. "What have you been up to?"

"Hey, my man!" Marcia's husband, Rick said, raising his hand for me to give him a high five. "So, I heard the mulled wine kiosk is opening in five."

Before we could even get further into a conversation, I looked at Leland and the hot chocolate he was still drinking. "I think mulled wine sounds great," I told him. "And we can come back here a little later on." In all truthfulness, I just wanted to get away from them. I wasn't ashamed of my bisexuality, or what I had with Leland, but I didn't want the million questions.

This was the first time I'd been with someone during the Christmas period in a while. It was nice, because there was an almost guaranteed level of having someone to share a bed with, and that filled me with all the happiness.

We took a lap around the town center, checking in on my stall before getting our helping of mulled wine. We were told to pace ourselves on it because a little could get us very drunk. Of course, the only rules I ever followed were the instructions to baking delicate pastries.

After a couple cups of wine, we were arm in arm, giggling with each other, right until Leland's mother caught us both and put us on grandma watching duty. And I learned that grandma carried a hip flask of whisky.

ELEVEN

LELAND

As a kid, the Christmas fair was huge. It didn't seem so big as an adult. I could drink—and drink I did, the mulled wine. And I ate the beef stew with a small bread roll to fill my belly. Marcus won me a giant teddy bear, humorously too big to carry. I think he might've actually bribed the ring toss people to get it for me.

We cuddled close on a single chair together, right beside my grandma, who was too busy pretending we didn't see her adding whisky to her coffee. We were all waiting for the nativity production to begin. A man in a Santa suit was hushing the crowd.

Each year, it was the same production, and each year, I

loved it more. It put the entire town in the spirit, more so than the giant fir tree covered in ornaments and lights.

Between the slight intoxication, and the comfort of sitting on Marcus's lap, I'd truly found a happiness I never wanted to let go of. Everything in the air was magical, especially the scent of spices and cinnamon. Although that was possibly from the food truck serving fresh, hot, deep fried apple pies and dusting them with a crazy number of spices.

"You think I could've played Santa?" Marcus whispered in my ear, jolting me gently with a single knee jitter.

I knew he turned the role down, just like my father had. The role was a speaking role, they were narrating the entire nativity. But before that, they'd been listening to children sat on their knees as they told them all their Christmas wishes and wants.

"Well, you're my Santa," I said, almost slipping. I wrapped my arms tighter around him.

"So, are you going to tell me what you want for Christmas?"

"I've already got it." My wishlist was complete. I had an endless supply of gingerbread, whether that was gingerbread people, or gingerbread cheesecakes. And I had an extremely hot man in my life who was willing to play Daddy for me. "What do you want for Christmas?"

His knee stopped jiggling me. "I've already got it."

"There's your brother," Grandma said. "Have you met

his girlfriend? Apparently, she roped him into it."

I hadn't even noticed him, dressed as one of Santa's elves. He was pushing across the stage with another elf. A girl, I assumed that was his girlfriend. "I guess now we know why he's been avoiding us all day," I said. Turning to Marcus, I pressed my face against his cheek, feeling the slur of alcohol in my mouth.

"Now, if you were one of my elves, maybe I'd actually contemplate being Santa," he said, squeezing his face back against mine. "I really can't wait to get you back to the apartment later." His hand sliding up through the back of my coat. I wiggled around, trying to escape his cold touch. "But we have to dismantle the stand before we can go back."

"We should leave early," I whispered loudly.

"Don't even think about it," my mom's voice came down on me from above. "You'll sit and enjoy the play. Your father has to, so you do too."

I looked behind to see my father with a folded newspaper in hand. "She's right," he said. "Although, I'm only staying because I'm driving everyone back home."

My mom let out chuckle. "I deserve every cup of mulled wine. For one thing, it's the holidays, and another—" a burp interrupted her. She quickly placed a hand to her mouth as dad and grandma chuckled.

In some of my wildest dreams, I'd dreamed of a moment when I would be sitting on the knee of someone I was dating at a big event. My family would be there, of course, and everyone would be full of cheer. I just always thought that would stay in my dreams.

Marcus wrapped an arm around me, squeezing me as if he was letting me know he was still there. I snuggled into him, appreciating the connection.

I just wanted to get back to my apartment and out of my bulky winter clothes. It was like having thick pillows between us, keeping us apart from each other.

As the evening went on and things were being packed away, my mom pulled me aside, away from Marcus.

"What does he like?" she asked.

"What do you mean?"

She tutted. "You know, I want to get him a gift for Christmas day when he comes over."

"Mom, it's fine, I don't think he's got you anything," I told her. "Inviting him was nice on its own."

My mom squinted, staring at me. I could see the slight intoxication in her eyes and the flushed pink on her cheeks. "Well, I've bought your brother's girlfriend something, so I need to get him a gift."

Cautiously glancing around, Marcus caught my eye and waved. He was dismantling the stand with help from my dad. "In his apartment, he collects these small snow globes, and they're all inside a glass cabinet."

She cooed. "Snow globes. How precious. Well, I don't know what I can do with that information on short notice, but it gives me something to work with." She gave me a firm nod, almost knocking the snug winter hat off her head.

I hadn't even got him a gift, and he'd got me two. One giant teddy, and one smaller pig teddy. Although it could be argued that I gave him my body, and that was probably the greatest gift I could give to him.

Once everything was packed away and stored for the next town event, Marcus and I went back to my apartment, with my incredibly large new teddy. And as soon as we were both through the door, we began stripping clothes from each other.

"What do you want for Christmas?" I asked, putting a pause to the action.

"You."

"No, no, no. I'm being serious. You have to say something. So, what do you want?"

He brushed a hand through my hair, tucking it behind my head. "I'm being serious. I don't want anything. Moments like this, where we both feel what each other's bodies want. That's all I want for Christmas, and New Year, and Valentine's, and St. Patrick's Day, and—"

"I have an idea, actually," I said, holding a finger and pressing it against his mouth. "But you'll have to wait until Christmas day."

He opened his mouth to suck on my finger. I moved it away, giggling. "That brings me to my question," he said. "Are you sleeping at mine or am I sleeping here on

Christmas Eve?"

"You have a Christmas tree," I said.

"That small plastic thing," he snickered. "You're right, but it's not a proper tree." He turned his head. "Maybe next year we can have a real tree."

He'd said what I was thinking. I wasn't trying to plan my life away, but I also wasn't planning on letting this feeling slip between my fingers either. "Again, your place or mine?"

"Your place is bigger," he said. "We could put a tree over there, right by the window."

It felt natural for the both of us to get lost in planning like this. Almost like we'd been waiting years to do it. And do it, sexually, we had been waiting years.

"I'll hold you to that," I said.

"Good. Put it in your calendar."

If I had a calendar, I would've added it. I'd just have to keep a strong mental note. Although I doubt I would easily forget it. He'd promised, and I always remembered promises.

He chased me around the room, trying to get me naked.

Jumping on the bed, I told him the floor was lava. He immediately perished on the ground in a dramatic flourish. He threw a hand up in the air and made gargling noises with his mouth.

"Nooooo," I reached out for his hand.

"Save yourself," he said, fake choking.

I sighed, rolling around on the comforter on my bed,

collecting it up and cocooning myself. "Who's gonna eat my ass now?"

Everything was quiet, he didn't respond to my question, although I suppose he was playing dead.

"Ragh!" he let out, slowly standing.

It was a mistake to roll myself up so tightly in the comforter.

He clawed his monster hands at the bed.

"Daddy, save me!"

"I can only be saved by—" he said, flopping on the bed. "Eating ass."

I rolled out of the comforter in speed, already slipped out of my underwear and presenting my ass in the air like a reward, ready to be claimed. My back keeping an arch, I wiggled my ass.

"Good boy," he said, giving my bum a tap with an open palm. "I think I'm feeling much better."

He ate my ass like someone who knew how to scoop pudding from the cup without leaving a drop. He went in with his tongue, fingers, and at one point, I almost felt a knuckle. My body was relaxed out on the bed, the buzz of alcohol still in my bed, letting more of the playfulness out.

It wasn't long until I begged him to fuck me.

He did. Slowly. My ass up, my back arched, my head in the pillow with one hand on my head, another on my back. He spread my legs and spread pleasure with it. Each pump of his cock in me had me clenching the bedsheets harder, screwing them up into my fists, pulling them up from the corners of the mattress.

"Cum on me," I begged.

Stretching out on my back, his head by mine. "On you?" he asked through labored breaths.

"Make me your gingerbread man," I whispered. "Put your icing on me."

His legs buckled, thrusting harder. His breathing shallow in my ear. "Oh. Fuck."

"Did you—"

"No, no, that did something for me," he said.

"You like that?" I asked, following the rhythm of his body against mine. "You want to squirt your icing all over me?"

"Yes!" With the pressure of his weight on my body, he pushed himself up. "You're my little gingerbread boy, and I'm gonna decorate you."

"Do it!"

He pulled out and gave my ass another tap. "On your face."

I was ready to be decorated by his sweet body icing. I kneeled in front of him, looking up at his pumped up, sweaty body. He removed the condom and tapped my face with his hot cock before beating fast.

"I'm ready," I said, closing my eyes and opening my mouth.

Several hot pumps hit my face, followed by his cock, like

he was using it as an icing bag he placed individual pumps of cum on me. I took a little of it on my tongue, smacking my lips and enjoying the delicious hard work he'd put into me.

He didn't realize until cleaning me off that I'd already came while he was fucking me, and there was now a wet patch on the bedding. He gave me a kiss and a cuddle. "You got all excited," he said.

"You make me excited," I said, pouting.

"You make me more excited," he said.

We went back and forth until we got into a tickle fight. I lost because I ran away from him.

It was the first night we'd get together where he didn't have to be awake super early in the morning. Since the bakery wasn't open on Sunday.

After spending all that energy on fucking and playing, we were far too tired to stay awake any longer. But that was fine, because he wasn't going anywhere, and neither was I.

TWELVE

MARCUS

I woke to a cool air tickling across my body. And then I heard him giggling.

On the floor, Leland was laid on his large teddy, wearing a white onesie, covered in a snowman print.

"Hey," I called out to him, pulling the comforter up my body. "What time is it?"

"Noooo," he said, swinging his entire body around to keep my sleepy eyes from seeing what he was doing. "Go back to sleep."

The one day of the week I was afforded to sleep in, and I made it to 8 A.M. which was good, since we'd fallen asleep early-ish last night. It was easy to fall asleep beside Leland.

He filled me with the right amount of excitement and relaxation for my body to even think of sleeping.

"I was going to make breakfast," he said, putting everything he'd been doing inside of a plastic bag. "I can make toast, and I can make coffee. Or there's some OJ in the fridge. You actually brought that."

Hugging the comforter up to my body, I climbed out of bed, completely naked under the comforter. "You really want to make me breakfast?" I asked, concerned. "Because if you ask me, I should be the one doing that."

"Relax," he said, tackling me with a hug and pushing me back on the bed. He stood, dusting off his hands, looking down at me grinning. "I've got this. You can either have your toast with butter, or jelly. And it might be a tiny bit burned, I don't know the settings on this toaster."

With my hands behind my head, I just nodded. "Gimmie what you got."

Watching Leland work the appliances in the apartment felt like it was his first time touching any of them. He caught me staring. "I usually buy breakfast on the way to work in city," he said.

"You're the one who offered it," I said.

"This is when you call me a good boy, and then you ask if I need any help."

I tutted. "Now you've said that, I think I might see how this turns out."

It turned out fine. The toast, only a little burned was

good. The coffee, however, was bad. I still told him he did a good job and he asked if I'd wanted a second cup of the weak coffee water, he'd sorta-kinda brewed.

We had the day to ourselves. I gave in to every one of Leland's whims. Everything he wanted to do today; we were doing it. We started with games on the consoles, followed by cuddles, a dance party to Christmas songs, and then he offered to make lunch as well.

"You've done enough," I said, pulling him into my arms as we sat together on the comfy beanbags. "Why don't I make us a pie?"

"A pie?" he asked, gasping, and looking around at all the nonexistent people int he apartment. "I love pie. Are we talking fruit pie, meat pie, fish pie, or like—what other pies are there?" his mouth turned to a frown. I gave him a quick peck. "Is this that thing when people refer to pizza as pie, or do you mean pie?"

"A real pie," I told him. "But we'll have to go to the bakery for ingredients."

"Can I come in my onesie?" he stood, giving me a twirl. "It has a hood." He demonstrated, pulling it over his face. There was an orange cone stuffed with fluff as a carrot for a nose.

"You can cum in whatever you want," I teased, reaching out to grab his bum.

I chased him around after that with him wiggling his bum for me to grab.

Hunger got the better of us and we made it to the bakery.

Usually, we made sweet pies in the bakery, but on occasion, I'd make myself a savory pie for lunch or dinner.

I sat Leland down in the kitchen, in front of a mixing bowl for the short crust pastry. He wanted to help, and I'd walked enough people through mixing a short crust pastry.

I was busy getting the beef out of the freezer. "I have beef chunks, we can have a beef pie with onion and red wine, in gravy," I said.

He already had flour on his nose. "And we can make a sweet one too, right?"

"What type do you want?" I asked. "A cream pie?"

Immediate eruption of giggles came out of him. "Not sure if that makes me more hungry or horny?"

"Hungry," I told him. "Because it would break a thousand health violations for us to fuck in here."

He pouted. "I suppose you have a point." And somehow, he had more flour on his face now. "And I want an apple pie, your version, those apple pie slices last night were amazing."

Staring into his big eyes, I obviously couldn't say *no.* "Once you've had my apple pie, you might just fall in love with me." Immediately, my mouth sealed shut. I'd said the L-word. *Love.*

"You could try," he said, biting down on his lip. "I'd like to see you try, at least."

I wondered if he wanted me to try to make him fall in

love with me. Because I was almost there, the nervous pit in my stomach of wanting to say those words to him, it opened, and swallowed me back in time. Almost like I was back in high school, and I plucked the courage to ask someone out. Then my first kiss. I had all those feeling snow, again, in my belly. I wondered if he did too.

"How am I doing with the pastry?" he asked, smacking the end of the wooden spoon against the bowl. "I think I got it all mixed."

"Yeah—you—" it was a mess. He wasn't born to be a baker, or come anywhere near a kitchen, but he looked so proud of making his mess inside the bowl, and only getting one-tenth of it on the counter. "You're almost there."

"What else can I do?" he asked. "I feel like this might be my second calling. I mean, I love accounting and numbers, but it doesn't compete to getting your hands—or a spoon stuck into a mixing bowl and making something."

I tsked playfully. "You know, if there was a job opening, I might just employ you."

"That would be a bad decision," he said, immediately shutting me down. "Firstly, our sexual chemistry is just so far off the charts, we couldn't work together. And secondly, I don't like to wait around for things to cook or have to be baked and checked on at a certain time. It seems exhausting."

He was right, it could become exhausting, but there were timers and more than anything, I truly enjoyed every aspect of baking. Plus, I didn't make a quarter as much mess as he did. "That's a damn shame," I said. "Guess you'll have to stick to your accounting job then."

"It's probably for the best. I'd hate for you to have to rename the bakery to *'Marcus & Leland, the baking extraordinaire'*," he said, painting the image with a hand gesture.

"I think the town is only big enough for one of us," I told him as I wrapped my arms around him. "Plus, there's already the cafe up the road I have to compete with some days."

Leland's mouth went to my neck, kissing me. "They have good coffee."

"Whose coffee is better?"

"Um—"

"No, no, there's no thinking," I said.

"Yours, of course, Daddy's coffee is the best."

"Good boy," I said, kissing him back. "Next step, you're gonna have to collect everything in the bowl into a ball, I think you might need a touch of water in there, just to help bring it together."

He gave me a two-finger salute. "Yes, Daddy."

Leland was fun. He could take orders, and he was so easy to be around. There was no arguing or frustration with him. Maybe it was the role play, the need to be taken care of. It helped me too, I never realized how much it was filling a part of my soul just to be there for him.

With the pastry, I rolled it out into two crimped tins, one for the apple pie, and another for the beef on the stove.

As our pies cooked in the oven, I sat with Leland. The comfort and bliss of quiet, just enjoying each other's company in quiet.

"Is it too early to talk about where we'll be staying on Christmas Eve?" I asked.

Leland sighed. "I honestly thought you'd have been sick of me in bed each night," he said.

"Well, you do move around a lot, but it's nice to wake up and see you there."

"You move around more," he said, furrowing his brow at me. "I think you kicked me last night."

"No, I didn't. Did I?" I asked, grabbing his hand and holding it. "I'm sorry, I—"

"Joking!" he chuckled. "I move around a lot because my insides are excited."

That was an answer I'd except, but I didn't mind him moving around at all. "Well, are we staying at yours, or mine?"

He answered immediately. "Yours," he said. "You have a Christmas tree and decorations."

"Decorations?"

"The snow globes."

A collection of snow globes passed on to me from my grandma, it was part of my inheritance. "Didn't I tell you about those?"

"No, I just—" his face flushed. "Was I not supposed to mention them?"

"Of course, you can," I said, before telling him the story of how my grandma was the collector. I added to them now and then whenever I saw them in giftshops, but they were more so there to memorialize her.

We took the finished pies upstairs to my apartment. I plated the savory beef pie for Leland in his pink, plastic bowl. He was giddy with excitement, almost bouncing on the chair at the table. The pastry wasn't half bad either. He certainly seemed to think so, asking me how well he'd done after every bite I took. He beamed with pride.

"I actually might need you to help me out during the week," I told him. "I have a huge list of desserts that need making."

"Of course, I'm a master baker, I'd love to help."

"A master what?" I asked, trying to illicit a certain response.

"Master baker."

"Master ba—"

"Oh!" he gasped. "You tried to get me to say a naughty word."

"Nooooo," I snickered. "What word was that?"

"Masturbator," he whispered.

He was right, I had tried to get him to say that. It almost sounded like what he'd said anyway. "I think that title is more fitting," I said, trying to find his foot beneath the table.

"But what do you think about spending more time with me and our off the charts sexual chemistry?"

Leland sighed, digging his adorable pink plastic piggy spork into the dish. "It's a tough call, on one hand, I get to spend more time with you, and on the other hand, I don't think I'll be able to not see you and think about being on my knees sucking your dick."

"I never said you'd have to stop thinking that," I said. "But it might be distracting."

"You think?" he sighed, shaking his head. "It's all I can think about."

"I feel you. You're all I can think about as well. Diving between those two peaches and giving you my cream."

His little tongue poked out to wet his lips. "Why didn't I ask for peaches and cream for dessert?" he whispered.

"That can be second dessert. But only if you manage to eat all of that first." I'd already finished mine. And now, I was trying to be a good example. Or so the online articles I'd read said.

"You're getting the hang of this Daddy thing."

High praise. "And if not, no dessert, and definitely no second dessert."

"You're really gonna fit in with my family at Christmas dinner," he said, spooning the pie into his mouth.

Equally high praise. I wanted to get along with his family. They all liked me, but now, it was different because I was dating Leland. I'd probably have to bring another dessert to dinner. I still had a couple days to think about that, and until then, I'd make the most of my day off with Leland.

THIRTEEN

It was Christmas day and I'd been awake since I felt Marcus move in the middle of the night. I couldn't wake him, he'd had an incredibly busy day yesterday, becoming his own version of Santa. I don't know what he was named, but I knew he delivered desserts to all the people in all the houses to make sure they had the perfect desserts for their Christmas meals.

And as soon as it turned 6 A.M. I jumped on him, shaking him awake. He barely even moved, only lifting an arm to try to swipe me under it and pull me to his chest. It didn't work, I had a surprising amount of energy. It was like those stories you hear when a parent saves their child through adrenaline, that was me, but with energy on Christmas morning. I never grew out of it. Nor would I want to grow out of it.

Today, I could say that my Christmas wishlist was complete. Santa outdid himself this year.

Marcus rubbed at his eyes and yawned while I continued to shake him.

"Come cuddle," he yawned.

I was too excited to lay still long enough to consider cuddles. "I want you to open you present!"

"My present?" he asked, perked up.

Shoving the small, wrapped present in front of him. "It's not much, but there's a lot to it," I told him.

He pulled the bow from it; it was a premade bow with sticky tape on the back. He stuck it to my forehead. "I didn't get you anything to open," he said, hesitating as his fingers worked around the paper, looking for somewhere to tear.

The gift was a blank check book with little stubs he could tear out to redeem things from. They were already prewritten in with the things I would do for him. They ranged from sex, to cuddles, and massages. I also decorated them with little piggy stickers I had laying around in the bottom of a box.

"I love it," he said, pulling me in by the head and kissing me.

"And you already gave me your gift," I said under the strain of his body pulling me down on him. "The teddies."

I reached over to the side of the bed I'd been sleeping on, grabbing the two teddies he'd got me, and Oinky, who I would never leave out of the collection.

Marcus let go of me, flicking through the checkbook, he pulled one out. "I want to redeem this one."

"Take a shower with me," I read aloud.

Since Marcus had been spending more time at my apartment, he'd brought over a couple of his things, including the gingerbread smelling body wash. I'd almost used it all, and I'd even got a little of it in my mouth accidentally. It wasn't harmful, at least it small doses, but it didn't taste anything like gingerbread.

Marcus undressed me from the onesie in the bathroom. He took every care of my body as he ran his hand down me, removing my t-shirt and underwear. It was probably strange of me to tell him about my role play fantasies, but he really enjoyed doing it with me, sometimes, he did it without me even prompting him.

I stood, covering my dick with a hand while he was in front of me, teasing me with his sexy body in a pair of black briefs. I could barely make out the head of his dick inside them.

"After this, I'll make us some breakfast," he said, turning the shower on. He dipped his hand under the water, feeling the temperature.

"I already promised my mom we would go up to the house for breakfast," I said. "Is that ok?"

"Of course, I'm ready to do whatever you want." He pulled his hand away, soaking wet, he wiped it down my chest. "I think we might have to wait for the water to get warm."

I kissed him, placing two fingers inside his waistband and yanking them down his thighs. "Your turn!"

He let it happen, placing his hands on his hips as if presenting his boner jump out of the briefs. "Nice boys ask permission first."

"I am a nice boy!" I said, trying to pull his brief back up, but his dick was in the way.

Chuckling to himself, he pulled me, wrapping his nice warm body around mine. "I know you are."

In the shower, once the water was warm, he took care of my body with a soft sponge and an endless number of bubbles. He had me back against his chest, transferring the body wash bubbles from me to him. I had my hands on his body, it was almost a secret, the fact both our dicks were hard but neither of us were touching them.

His hands were first. All the way down to my dick. I copied him, using the soap as lube to jerk his cock as fast as I could.

"Oh, baby—I'm gonna—" he pulled me in and came on me. His hand and pace grew harder and faster as he tugged on my cock. I came seconds after, trying to compete with his spurt of cum up my body, but instead, mine was more of a dribble from the end of my dick.

It was a nice way to start the day. Now, I was clean inside and out.

I wore one of my Christmas sweaters, and Marcus wore a red sweater with two candy canes on the front. He joked and said that the two candy canes represented me and him; our dicks. I told him not wear it because my grandma had been knitting him his own sweater, and she'd probably ask him to take that one off to turn it.

My family were all awake, even my brother Harry and his girlfriend, Naomi. It was 8 A.M. when we arrived, and the sweet smell of turkey roasting in the oven welcomed us. There was also the smell of bacon too, which wasn't as welcoming since I'd committed my allegiance to Oinky, and when pigs rose up against humans, I'm sure my life would be spared.

Marcus brought three desserts with him, one which my mom had ordered, and two more because he felt bad for being invited for Christmas dinner. And I brought a small bag with my wrapped gifts.

"Merry Christmas," my mom said, welcoming us both. "You smell lovely. Did you sleep in the bakery?"

"It's a new body wash," I told her.

Before I got the chance to go around everyone, my grandma summoned Marcus to her, snapping her fingers until he sat beside her in the living room. I left him to give my mom and dad their gifts. A bottle of scotch whisky for my dad, and a collectable tea set for my mom.

Everyone, except for grandma was at the dining table. Harry and his girlfriend, in a world of their own, whispering to each other and giggling. Young love, I was jealous of it.

"Pancakes!" my mom hollered.

"Mrs. Jenkins," I heard Marcus call out. "You need any help?"

He walked through the dining room in a brand-new cream and red Christmas sweater. It had his name on it and a giant knitted Santa face in the center.

"No, no, you take a seat, hon," she said. "And I told you, call me Cora."

Marcus sat beside me, a wild wide grin on his face.

"What did she say?" I whispered to him.

"You told me she was going to burn it, like you said."

My dad snickered from the head of the table. "She's not kidding," he said. "I hope you didn't leave it with her. She'll find a match somewhere and the place will be up in smoke."

"Seriously?" he asked.

"No," my dad continued, belly chuckling. "But if you did give it to her, I wouldn't expect to see it back again."

I still had to give grandma her gift. So, I left Marcus in the dining room and joined my grandma in the living room. She was still in her nightdress with a blanket over her legs.

"Your boyfriend is nice," she said.

"He's not my—" I paused, turning to see if anyone was listening. "Thank you."

"You know, I got to see him take off his sweater. Have

you seen his tattoos?" she let out a playful gasp. "If you don't snatch him up, I will."

"I might have to talk about that with him," I said. "I got you a present."

"Was it that man?" she asked, grabbing my arm and shaking it.

"No, grandma. Why don't you open it?" The last gift in the bag.

She looked at it and scoffed. "Now you know very well I don't do well with finnicky stuff like that. You'll have to open it for me."

Opening it for her, I saw happiness fill her up. It was only yarn, something she needed for her knitting, but I knew it meant the world to her. She gave me a hug, patting me down almost.

"You need to eat more," she said. "I can feel your bones."

I doubted she could feel them through the thickness of the sweater.

We all sat and ate breakfast pancakes in the dining room. People, not naming anyone, had bacon with theirs. I stick with the sweet options, honey and strawberries. I barely heard a word from Harry and Naomi as they went upstairs after breakfast was over.

In the living room, under the grand Christmas tree, my mom pulled out two boxes. They were upcycled shoe boxes she'd decorated with wrapping paper. "So, I didn't know what to get you, both of you. I made up some boxes, like I would if we were doing Christmas stockings."

Inside my box, there was a pink mug with cartoon pigs on it, a new calculator, candies, and a gingerbread scented candle.

"You know, the calculator because you're starting your new job with your dad," she said.

"I love it!" My importantly, I love the mug.

Marcus's box had a snow globe with a cabin inside, but with glitter. He also had candies, and a brownie scented candle. He glanced at me when he pulled the snow globe out. "Thank you, Mrs. Je—Cora."

"And I know you have your bakery, but when I saw those candles, I knew they'd be perfect for you."

There was also a slight sadness there as he looked away and picked his gaze up to me again. "It's perfect," he said. "Are you sure I can't help you out in the kitchen?"

She chuckled. "You're a guest. If you want to help, I'll get you to set the table later. For now, I think you have a friend who needs entertaining." She gestured to grandma, staring at Marcus. It felt like he was being fed to the wolf in *Little Red Riding Hood.*

Fortunately for me, she was only occupied for about fifteen minutes before something caught her attention on the TV.

I took Marcus to the bedroom where all my childhood things were. It was the smallest room now, since rooms had been swapped, and I wasn't living at home, but my mom didn't want to box everything. She kept it made up in case I ever stayed over. It was almost like a shrine with pictures of me all throughout middle school and high school on the walls.

"You look adorable," he said.

I sat him on the small, single bed. "I can't believe I told my mom about the snow globe thing."

"I thought it was cute," he said, holding my hand as I paced the small space in the room. "I think you're cute. Sit next to me. I have something I want to ask you."

Now, more than ever, I wanted to pace. I knew nothing good could come from being told someone wants to ask you something. "Ok. I—"

He pulled me into his arms, effectively sitting on his lap. "You can say *no*, of course, but I—I want to call you my boyfriend."

"Oh."

"So, my question is, will you be my boyfriend?"

It was what I wanted, so why was it difficult to speak?

"Obviously, moving too fast, this is all new for me but I—"

"Yeah," I said. "My boyfriend. It has a nice ring to it. Like, oh my boyfriend owns a bakery."

"Or, oh, my boyfriend is an accountant."

I shook my head and hummed. "Being a baker is way cooler."

"Being a *master* baker is cooler," he teased, digging his fingers into my hips to tickle me.

"You're a master baker!"

"Don't make me master bake all over you," he chuckled.

I was open to him master baking all over me, but maybe not in this room where all my family could probably hear. "I can't wait to tell everyone," I said, jumping from his lap and racing downstairs.

In the living room, my brother and his girlfriend were stood in the middle of the room. "Naomi is pregnant," he announced, blowing any hype my announcement would've made out of the water.

My mom screamed with excitement and my dad plugged fingers in his ears at the noise.

"Congrats," I said, my grip becoming tight on Marcus's hand.

Marcus kissed my cheek. "I love you."

Oh boy.

AAA

AAA

FOURTEEN

MARCUS

I'd said it. I wasn't going to take it back. I just saw the look in his eyes, and the way his teeth sank into his bottom lip. He whispered it back to me and pulled me into a hug. I didn't really listen to what his brother had said, but the entire family were screaming it moments later.

We barely got another moment alone together until we were setting the table.

"Don't worry," I whispered to him. "We won't have that problem."

"Which one?" he asked, butting his lips into a thin smile as he made shifty eyes, looking around the empty dining room.

"You know, getting pregnant," I said.

He giggled, placing a hand on his belly. "Put a baby in me."

"Oh, what have I—" his mother said, turning on her heel at the dining room door.

We burst into laughter together.

Walking back into the dining room with some decorative pieces for the table, his mom smiled at the both of us. "It's a shock," she said. "I'm happy for them, but I'm too young to be a grandmom. Anyway, no more surprises today please." She flicked back her hair.

"Mom," he said. "Me and Marcus are actual boyfriends now, so just in case you were keeping tabs."

Her eyes lit up. She walked over to me, smiling ear-to-ear. She pinched at my cheek. "Does that mean I get a family discount at the bakery?"

"Of course."

She wrapped me in a hug, patting and rubbing my back. "I approve," she said. "All we need now is a glass of champagne, or at least a mimosa. You know, vitamin C is incredibly important in your diet during the winter season."

"I could go for a mimosa," I said.

"Mom, if you had mimosas, you should've served them with breakfast," Leland said. "I would've killed for a mimosa this morning."

"Well, I was saving the champagne, but now that your brother is having a child and you've got a boyfriend, I think it's calls for celebration," she said. "Now, finish setting the table. I want that good cutlery used. You know the ones, slim handle, a little heavy on the ends." She nodded with her instruction, demonstrating with gestures about the cutlery she wanted. I didn't know; this was my first time in the house.

Leland's mom got the mimosas and a single champagne flute of orange juice for Naomi. We toasted their pregnancy, and I toasted a second time with Leland in secret.

His family were incredible company. My family were usually busy, we often arranged an activity during the day, followed by a meal made at whatever club my parents were part of. It was nice to have the full family experience. Not only was there warmth from them, but a physical heat from food being made. And I enjoyed that feeling more than anything else, it reminded me of where I liked to be the most.

I'd texted my parents and sister, and I knew for certain they were all off being busy with something. My sister was probably on a hike, and my parents were probably golfing. Neither of them had gotten back in touch with me, which wasn't a foreign concept, that's just how we operated.

After the large dinner, which I was told numerous times I couldn't help with, we made room for dessert.

We left before the Monopoly board was pulled out. Leland insisted we leave before that. Apparently, he had a competitive side he didn't want me to see just yet. I didn't know if I could break the truth to him that I'd already seen his competitive side while we played games on his console.

We took our gift boxes and half a gingerbread cheesecake back with us.

"I love you," he said, unprompted as I set the items down on the kitchen counter. "I—I don't know what it is, but you've been on my mind so much, for years."

Embracing him, squeezing him against my chest. "I love you too." And there was something to what he'd said about being on his mind for all those years. He'd been there too, on mine. "You know, I've never once regretted kissing you. Even if I tried to blame it on the alcohol sometimes."

"Wait," he paused. "You thought kissing me was a mistake?"

"No, I'd never say that, and if I did, then it would've been my greatest mistake," I told him. "Actually, my greatest mistake was something I did experimenting with cupcake flavors back in culinary school, but you know, second best greatest mistake has a nice ring to it."

Leland giggled, fighting my torso with tickles.

It didn't have the same effect as it did while I wore my brand-new Christmas sweater. It was so thick, and incredibly warm, I could've lived in it. It didn't surprise me, Leland loved his so much, I wondered what he'd wear once the holiday season was over.

My phone buzzed in my pocket, cutting off the playing.

A video call from my parents.

In the sun, my mom held the phone inches from her face. "*Hey son,*" she said. "*We're just on the caddy back to the club.*"

"Merry Christmas," I said.

"*Merry Christmas,*" they called back to me.

"I want to introduce you to my boyfriend," I told them. It wasn't the way I wanted it, but after all the warmth Leland's family had shown me today, I was taken over. "This is Leland." I shoved the phone in his face for them to see him. He was a rabbit in headlights, wide eyed and startled.

"*Oh, is that Cora's boy?*" my mom asked, adjusting her glasses as she stared at him.

"Yeah," I said, turning the phone back to me. "We look forward to you coming back so you can properly meet each other."

"*Sounds like a great idea, son,*" my dad called out. "*We'll talk later, yeah. We're almost back at the club.*"

They hung up before I could say *bye*. It was fine, but after the day I'd had, surrounded by love and warmth, I felt the distance my family had always exhibited. After the call, I felt I had to explain it to him. All he did back was hug me, and he stayed hugging me until I picked him up and carried him over to the bed.

"I'm so tired," I yawned.

He stuck a finger in my yawning mouth. "Oopsie."

"You're lucky I really like you," I said, before feeling a

second yawn coming in my jaw.

"I thought you said love."

"Thank you so much for being you." I placed a hand behind the back of his head and stroked a thumb across his cheek. "Thank you for showing me what you like, and for allowing me to be part of it."

Nuzzling his head into my head, he made sure for my hand to stroke his entire head. "It's because you made me feel comfortable," he said. "I wouldn't have been able to tell you any of that without feeling comfortable."

"You know, I searched the internet for tips on how to do it," I confessed. The post-food sleep haze was taking over me, it was almost like being drunk. "I realized a lot of what I was doing was good play. Nurturing, giving you the space to regress and do your thing, no judgement, or anything."

"I never do it with anyone else," he whispered. "It's a space I only go into alone, but it was easy to welcome you into it."

We cuddled, arm in arm, falling asleep with each other until I snored and woke myself and him up.

Leland stretched like a cat after lounging in the sun all day. "Every time I open my eyes and see you there, I'm grateful my Christmas wish came true."

"It's Christmas," I said. "You can tell me your wish now."

There was contemplation in his eyes, a decision was

being made. "There were two wishes," he said, holding up two fingers.

"Ok, and I'll tell you mine, if you tell me yours," I said, although I didn't have a Christmas wish, but if I did, I'm pretty sure it would've been granted with the fortunate situation with Leland in bed.

"I wanted an endless supply of gingerbread, in all forms, gingerbread lattes, gingerbread men, gingerbread loaves," he said, listing them off. "And I wanted someone to play with me."

Humming loudly, I squinted, staring into his eyes. "I guess you wished for me then."

"It sounds funny, but I think I might have."

I pulled him on top of me. He laid his head on my chest.

"What was your wish?" he asked.

"My wish was to have someone I could feed my endless supply of gingerbread too, and also someone to play with." I was a baker, so I could have an endless supply of all his favorite gingerbread flavored baked goods. The plaything was something we both realized was a long time coming for the both of us.

It had only taken three years to get to this place, and it came at the perfect time. I came out and accepted my bisexuality this year, something I hadn't done when we'd first kissed. He moved back to town, and I caught him spying. It was almost fate, except playing the waiting game. I didn't mind playing the waiting game, all that mattered was finding someone I was comfortable with. Leland was that person. We meshed on so many levels that we were almost intertwined.

"Love you."

"Mean it?" he asked.

"Like ninety-nine percent."

"Good enough," he snickered. "Love you too."

EPILOGUE

LELAND

Three Months Later

People always say that same-sex couples move too quick. That was absolutely correct. Once, I invited a guy over to hook-up with and he ended up spending two months at my apartment. With that in mind, it took Marcus three months to finally move into my apartment above the accountancy office.

The apartment he had above the bakery was still there, and he had no intentions of letting it out to anyone since he was keeping all the snow globes he'd accumulated there. I didn't even realize at the time when I looked at the shelf, but that thing had tiers. There were so many of them. Plus, he wanted to keep them there so his grandma's spirit could look over the building.

It was a Sunday, the one day of the week we got to spend the entirety of together.

"I think we might need to get a second wardrobe," Marcus said as he went from my closet to the dresser. "Babe."

Absorbed in my game, but with an eye on him just in case he moved anything. And since we'd invested in the comfiest loveseat sofa, I never wanted to leave it. "Yeah?"

"I'm not sure if all your onesies need hanging up in the closet," he said.

My finger slapped on the pause button. "I'm sorry."

"Got your attention now," he said, winking at me. "Come help me make room for my clothes."

Dragging myself from the sofa, I slumped against him. "You don't need clothes," I said. "I mean, you need clothes to work, but you don't *need* clothes. In fact, I prefer you without them. So, we can actually get rid and donate all of these."

"If I'm naked all the time, then you have to be naked all the time too," he said.

I gasped, a hand to my mouth. "But when will I wear my onesies?"

"And if I don't have clothes on, then how will we be able to undress each other?"

He made an excellent point. And the onesies didn't need hanging. The only thing in the closet that needed to be on a hanger were my work shirts. Although I would've just folded them and put them in a drawer, but it was apparently unprofessional to show up in front of clients with giant creases in your shirt.

We made the room for his things together. I liked seeing his things among mine. He filled the hole in the apartment. He'd slowly been bringing his things over since the first few nights when we started dating. It started with things he brought food over in, and then he left them there. Even the fridge was always stocked, which was good, because I'd forget to do that. I was someone who would see an empty fridge, tell myself I needed to go shopping, order takeout. Rinse and repeat each step every day because the same thing happened.

Marcus actually made food, from scratch, with raw ingredients. It was almost like I'd never seen it before, although I grew up in a household where my mom made as much as she could. But Marcus went above. He made pasta. Who knew fresh pasta wasn't hard and dry?

He got me involved in the process as much as he could, mentoring me in a way, being a guiding hand and a nurturing figure.

And each night, we took it in turns to choose something to watch. Although if I'd been a particularly good boy that day, meaning, I'd made the bed without asking, and not leaving a mess of clothes in a pile on the floor, then I was given control over the film choice. Which we never really made it the entire way through since I would get distracted just by being in his presence.

"I think we should get away for a weekend soon," he said. "Now that I'm officially moved in, we should do more couple things."

"Is this your way of asking if I want to go hiking?" I asked. He'd mentioned hiking a couple of times, and each time, I pretended to fall asleep.

"Maybe. But I just want to do things with you. I want to show you off to people."

I couldn't say *no* to that. I wanted to show him off too. And I had, on video calls to my friends in the city.

"In fact," he said, before I could answer him. "Why don't we plan to take a couple weeks off in the summer and go traveling."

"Europe?"

"Well, you did tell me you wanted to travel."

I had. And he'd remembered. That was one of the first things we'd talked about when he mentioned how well-traveled he was. "Italy is definitely on the list then," I said. "So, I can compare how your pizza tastes to their pizza."

"And if you're feeling like a good boy, you know what you'll say, right?"

"Yes, Daddy," I answered, pouting at him. "Your food is always the best. My favorite."

"You're my favorite," he said, grabbing me with his hands in grabby claws. I ran as he chased me around the apartment to grab at me and pretend to nibble on my body. "Oh, you are delicious." I went to bite him back. He held a finger up in front of my face. "No biting."

"But you did it to me."

"That's because—" I could tell he was struggling to think of a rule. "That's because I'm redeeming one of my tickets that say only, I can eat you, and you can't eat me."

"Noooo, that's not one of the tickets."

"Are you saying I'm a liar?"

Stumped by the audacity of the accusation. "No, I'd never call you a liar. Unless you were lying."

"Daddy doesn't lie."

"If that's true, then I have a question."

He pulled his tickling hands from my body. "Ask away."

"How much do you love me?"

"*The limit does not exist*," he said.

I burst into a fit of laughter.

"What?" he asked. "Did I get the *Mean Girls* quote right?"

"Yes, and I love you that much too."

THE END

Make sure to check to come back and visit Hinton, New Hampshire in the *My Little's Wishlist* series.

AUTHOR'S NOTE

Hello reader,

Christmas is my favorite time of year. The smells, the decoration, and most importantly, the food. I'm currently living in Madrid, Spain, inside the city center where they go crazy with Christmas decorations. I'll be posting pictures of the decoration once they're turned on. Outside my apartment, they've already got snowflake lights hanging above the street, but they haven't been turned on.

I hope you'll continue the journey through Hinton as we get cozy with more Daddies and littles.

A huge **THANK YOU** to my 'Book Baby' supporters on Patreon who get exclusive and behind-the-scenes content, as well as advanced reader copies.

Tonya Polk, Bruno Neves, Cassie Geiger, David-Eric Nikielski, Fancy Tiefenau, JustToni, Willow Thomas, Tina Marie, Janet Hunt.

I also want to thank Cathy Christmas for help with proofreading. You're a star!

And thank you for reading!

About the Author

JOE SATORIA is an MM romance author currently living in—who knows—anywhere in the world, really. He's a hopeful romantic—the hope being in his ability to one day find romance outside of fiction. And he's also a cat person—but deathly allergic to them.

If you can find me, follow me—I won't get a restraining order (this time).

If you love a good contemporary gay romance novel, I'll be serving it up to you from my favorite place in the world—my bed.

www.JoeSatoria.com